THE BOBBSEY TWINS
ON A HOUSEBOAT

"It's a houseboat," replied Bert Bobbsey

The Bobbsey Twins
on a Houseboat

By

LAURA LEE HOPE

GROSSET & DUNLAP
Publishers • New York

Published in 2004 by Grosset & Dunlap, a division of Penguin Young
Readers Group, 345 Hudson Street, New York, New York 10014.
GROSSET & DUNLAP is a trademark of Penguin Group (USA) Inc.
THE BOBBSEY TWINS® is a registered trademark of
Simon & Schuster, Inc.

Printed in the U.S.A.

ISBN 0-448-43757-0

1 3 5 7 9 10 8 6 4 2

CONTENTS

CHAPTER I

A BOAT FIRE

"OH, LOOK!" cried Freddie Bobbsey. "Somebody built a house right in the water!" The little blond-haired boy pointed his chubby finger straight ahead as the two sets of Bobbsey twins walked toward Lake Metoka.

"What is it?" Flossie asked, picking up the toy sailboat her six-year-old twin brother had dropped in his excitement.

"A houseboat!" replied Bert Bobbsey, their twelve-year-old brother.

"It's called the *Bluebird* and there's a sign on it," said Nan Bobbsey, whose brown hair and eyes closely resembled those of her twin brother, Bert. She rushed forward to read the wording and announced, "The boat's for sale!"

"Let's buy it!" said Freddie. "And live on it!"

"What do you do with a boat house, Nan?" asked Flossie, her golden curls blowing in the June breeze.

Nan's eyes twinkled as she looked at her little sister. *"Houseboat,* Flossie. And it's just what it sounds like—a small house built on a flat-bottom boat. Houseboats are made so they can sail on the water. Isn't that right, Bert?"

"They don't actually sail," said Bert, correcting his slender, pretty twin. "Houseboats are run by an engine nowadays."

"They must be fun!" exclaimed Flossie. "I'd like one for my dolls so I could take them sailing. Maybe I can put sails on my dollhouse."

Freddie chuckled. He was observing the houseboat with interest. "It even has a kitchen," he said, a happy expression in his bright blue eyes. Any thought of food was exciting to Freddie, and his family often teased him about his appetite.

"And a good stove," added Flossie. "Look at all the smoke coming out of that little window in the cellar!"

"You're right," said Bert, "but that's the hold of the boat—not the cellar. And the smoke's not coming from a stove. Say, there's a fire on board!"

"Whee!" shouted Freddie. "Let's put it out!" The small boy had been nicknamed "Little Fat Fireman" by his father some time before, because he loved to put out fires.

The four children raced to the dock where the houseboat was anchored. To their surprise they saw a middle-aged man fast asleep in a canvas chair, on the starboard deck of the boat.

His face was lightly tanned and underneath his hat they could see wisps of reddish-colored hair. Apparently he had gone to sleep while fishing, for a pole dangled from his hands.

Bert ran up the little gangplank leading from the dock to the boat and the other children followed. They jumped down to the deck and rushed over to the sleeping man.

Freddie could not wait for Bert to awaken him gently. "Mister!" he yelled in the man's ear. "Wake up! Your boat's on fire!"

The man's eyes flew open and he sprang to his feet. "Where?" he asked, looking at the twins in great surprise.

"Down in the hold!" Bert said quickly.

The man rushed inside the cabin. In a second he reappeared, holding two fire extinguishers.

"Here, boy," he said to Bert, handing him one of the extinguishers, "you come and help me. The rest of you stay up here!"

As Bert dashed after him, a disappointed look appeared on Freddie's face. In the past he had helped put out several small fires with some of his own assortment of toy apparatus.

"If I had my fire engine with the big tank and hose here, I could put this fire out in a minute," he said.

Soon the small twins and Nan could hear the *swish swish* of the fire extinguishers. They watched the clouds of smoke, which turned from gray to white.

"I'd better help them," insisted Freddie, dancing up and down with eagerness. He started to run inside, but Nan grabbed hold of his arm.

"This is one fire you'll have to miss, Freddie," she said. "You don't know where to go and you might get hurt."

The small twin reluctantly agreed that Nan was right. "But I'll learn," he said finally.

Meanwhile, Bert and the boat owner were working furiously to keep the flames from spreading. Within a few minutes they had them under control. The smoke grew thinner and then disappeared completely. Soon the fire fighters came on deck.

"It's out," Bert said with a grin, and the man added, "Yes, thanks to you youngsters. Nothing serious, fortunately. Some old, oily rags ignited."

"I'm glad you caught it in time," said Nan.

"I'm Mr. Enslow," the man said, wiping beads of perspiration from his thin face. "And you are—"

"We're the Bobbsey twins!" Flossie said.

"All of us!" Freddie added, and gave their names.

"Are you from around here?" Mr. Enslow asked.

"Yes, we live here in Lakeport," Nan replied. "Freddie wanted to try out his new sailboat, so we all came along for the launching."

"Last time Freddie went sailboating, he fell in," said Flossie.

"I did it on purpose!" Freddie spoke up. "I wanted to see if the water was deep enough so my boat would float."

Mr. Enslow laughed and suggested they all have some lemonade. He went to the galley and returned shortly with a pitcher, glasses, and a plate of cookies.

At this moment a voice from the gangplank called, "Hey, I want some, too."

Without turning around, the Bobbsey twins recognized the boy who came on board. He was Danny Rugg, a bully who was always playing mean tricks on them. Danny was Bert's age, but slightly taller and heavier. Nan introduced him to the owner of the houseboat.

As Mr. Enslow poured a glass of lemonade for him, Danny said loudly, "Glad you got that fire out. I was afraid you wouldn't hear me when I shouted to you."

"You shouted?" said Mr. Enslow, giving Danny a perplexed look. "The Bobbsey twins here woke me up."

Danny glared at the children, who said nothing, although they felt sure he had not even been near the boat.

When they finished their drinks, Mr. Enslow said, "Come, I'll show you around the *Bluebird.*"

He led his callers first into the main cabin. It was a spacious room filled with comfortable leather furniture. In one corner stood an old upright piano.

From this room a stairway led down to the hold, and a corridor ran to the rear of the boat. Off this corridor were four bedrooms, a bath, galley, and combination dining room-playroom.

"This is like my dollhouse!" Flossie exclaimed with glee. "But even nicer!"

Mr. Enslow now took them up an outside stairway to inspect the wheelhouse, where the boat's captain had his living quarters.

"This is nifty!" Bert said with enthusiasm, looking down at the small dinghy which was suspended from the side of the main deck.

Freddie was interested in the big anchor lying in the bow.

"Yes, it's a fine boat," Mr. Enslow agreed. "I bought it in Florida several years ago and I've never regretted it."

"Why are you selling it?" Freddie asked.

"Because my business has been transferred to the West and I can't take the boat with me.

A friend of mine in Lakeport was interested in buying the *Bluebird,* so I made the trip from Florida to show it to him. When I arrived he had already bought a houseboat. So, I'm trying to find another buyer," Mr. Enslow concluded.

"My father will buy it," Danny Rugg said boastfully. "He's got lots of money."

"I'm not looking for a rich man," said Mr. Enslow in a stern voice. "The previous owner was a very kind person. He made me promise that if I ever sold this houseboat it would be to someone who would be happy on the *Bluebird.*"

"Well, the Rugg family is just who you're looking for. I'm going to speak to my father right away," said Danny. With that, he ran down the steps, across the deck, and over the gangplank.

"We must be going, too," said Nan. "It's nearly suppertime. Thank you, Mr. Enslow, for the lemonade and for letting us go over the *Bluebird.*"

The boat owner invited the Bobbseys to visit him again soon.

"We'll be back," Flossie promised. "It's the bestest boat I ever saw."

The two sets of twins hurried off.

"I'm going to ask Daddy to buy the *Bluebird* before Danny's father does," Freddie declared.

"The *Bluebird* might be too expensive," Nan said thoughtfully. "And what would we do with a houseboat once we had it?"

"We could take a trip," replied Flossie. "My dolls like to go places." The others laughed at Flossie's remark. She was always worrying about her dolls' comfort.

The children quickened their steps and were back on their own street within a short time.

"I'm going to talk to Daddy and Mother first," said Flossie, starting to run toward their home.

"No, I am," insisted Freddie, catching up to his sister.

Mrs. Bobbsey was standing in the front yard showing Mr. Bobbsey some beautiful spring flowers which had recently bloomed. Flossie, dashing ahead of her twin, ran to her parents, shouting:

"Mother! Daddy! Buy us a boathouse!"

CHAPTER II

WONDERFUL NEWS

"A BOATHOUSE!" exclaimed the twins' tall, good-looking father. "What in the world would we keep in it, Flossie?"

Before the little girl could reply, Freddie ran across the front lawn, his blue eyes blinking with excitement.

"We got fired in the hole!" he shouted.

Bert and Nan, who now joined the group, laughed at Freddie's words. "What Freddie means," said Nan, "is that there was a fire in the hold of a houseboat we saw."

Mrs. Bobbsey, the twins' attractive, young mother, looked at her children and the corners of her mouth turned up in a smile.

"Please start at the beginning," she begged, laughing.

At that moment the front door opened and Dinah Johnson, the Bobbseys' plump cook, stood in the doorway. Dinah had been with the family for several years and had shared many of their adventures.

"Supper's going to get cold!" Dinah exclaimed, in a voice which pretended to scold. "You all coming in to eat it soon?"

"Shall we go?" invited Mrs. Bobbsey. "We can hear all about the boat and the fire at dinner."

During the meal the children told their parents about their afternoon's adventure.

"The *Bluebird*'s for sale, Dad," Bert said in conclusion, and the twins looked eagerly at their mother and father.

Mr. Bobbsey smiled broadly at Flossie. "I think I understand now, Little Sweet Fairy," he said, using his pet name for her. "The *Bluebird* is the 'boat house' you'd like me to buy."

"Yes. Oh, please, Daddy!" Flossie cried.

"But Danny Rugg's father may get there ahead of you," added Freddie. "You'd better hurry down to see it."

"That's right!" agreed Nan, and told her parents of the encounter with Danny aboard the boat.

Mr. Bobbsey made no comment for a few moments. Finally he looked at Mrs. Bobbsey with a wink and said, "Well, Mary, this might be the answer to our summer vacation. Let's look at the *Bluebird* after church tomorrow."

"Oh, Daddy!" the twins chorused, and Flossie ran around the table to give Mr. Bobbsey a bear hug.

The next day the family walked over to Lake Metoka. The twins eagerly led their parents up the gangplank of the houseboat and introduced Mr. Enslow, who was on deck.

Then Bert looked at Mr. Enslow anxiously. "Has Danny Rugg's father bought your boat yet?"

"No, I haven't seen him," the owner replied. "But I hardly think I'd be interested in any offer Mr. Rugg might make. His son isn't the type I'd like to have aboard my boat for long."

Mr. Enslow took Mr. and Mrs. Bobbsey on a tour of inspection, showing them the various cabins and explaining a little about the boat's operation. Flossie and Nan wandered into the room they had decided they would like to have. They especially admired the three bunks which were built into the wall.

Meanwhile, Freddie got Bert to take him down to the hold of the boat and look over the damage which the fire had done. At once Freddie pretended he was a fire inspector.

"You and Mr. Enslow are good firemen," he declared. "I see the ashes have been brushed up like they're supposed to be."

Bert grinned as they went back to the main deck. Nan and Flossie joined them and walked to where Mr. and Mrs. Bobbsey were talking with Mr. Enslow.

"Do you suppose Dad's decided to—to buy

the *Bluebird* so we can have a vacation on it?"
Nan whispered eagerly. The others did not
reply, because they were wondering the very
same thing.

In the past, the Bobbsey twins and their parents had spent many wonderful vacations together. Some of these came about because of
Mr. Bobbsey's business. He owned a large lumberyard and sawmill on the shore of Lake
Metoka, and sometimes took trips to buy lumber.

Once in a while the twins went to visit their
cousins. One of them, Harry, lived on a farm.

The other, Dorothy, lived at the seashore. A short time before, the Bobbseys had visited Snow Lodge, where the twins had solved a strange mystery.

Several of their adventures had included their big pet dog, Snap, who had once belonged to a circus, and Snoop, their cat, who was all black except for a patch of white under his chin.

Right now, the twins were eagerly watching their parents and Mr. Enslow as they talked in low voices. Finally, the men shook hands. The twins held their breath and then they noticed the twinkle in Mr. Bobbsey's eyes as he turned toward them.

"It's all settled," he announced. "We're going on a long voyage—aboard our new house-boat!"

What a chorus of happy shouts there was as the twins rushed over to their parents! And Flossie kept chanting gaily:

"We're going to live on the water! We're going to live on the water!"

"I wouldn't brag about owning that old tub," cried a scornful voice from shore.

The twins looked around to see Danny Rugg staring up at them, an unpleasant expression on his face. As if to prove he meant what he said, Danny picked up a rock and threw it toward the deck.

"Watch out!" shouted Bert. "Duck!"

Fortunately Danny's aim was bad, and the rock glanced off the cabin of the boat, then fell into the water with a loud splash. Bert, angered, started after the mean boy, but stopped as Danny disappeared in a near-by woods. It might take a long time to find him.

The children soon forgot the incident in their excitement about the boat. On the way

home they were bubbling over with questions
about the trip. When would they leave and
what should they take along? All talked at
once.

Finally Mr. Bobbsey said with a laugh, "One
twin at a time is all I can answer. We'll go in
about two weeks and your mother will arrange
about the clothes."

When they reached home, the twins ran to
Dinah, who was sitting in the back yard read-
ing the newspaper.

"Dinah!" Freddie shouted. "We bought the
houseboat!"

"You mean—one of those boats people *live*
on?" she asked in amazement.

"Yes!" exclaimed Flossie. "We're going on
a trip and you're going with us."

"Oh, no, not me!" said Dinah firmly. "You'll
never get me on a boat again! Not since I got
seasick in a fishing boat at one time."

"Oh, Dinah, you won't mind being on the
Bluebird," Flossie told her. "Our boat's not
the wobbly kind."

Everyone laughed and the family went inside the house to discuss the trip in more detail.
Mr. Bobbsey said he would have the *Bluebird*
overhauled and painted before their departure.

"Dad, may I ask Harry to go with us?" Bert
asked. His cousin was twelve also and fun.

"And Dorothy?" said Nan quickly.

"And Snoop and Snap," put in Flossie and Freddie together.

Their father nodded and Mrs. Bobbsey said, "I'll telephone the Meadowbrook Bobbseys and Dorothy's mother at the shore in the morning to find out."

Bert wanted to know what route his father planned to follow on the houseboat journey.

"I thought we might go down Lake Metoka to Lemby Creek," replied Mr. Bobbsey. "We haven't been in that direction for some time. From the creek we can enter Arrow Lake."

"Goody!" Flossie burst out. "That's where there's a big waterfall that bounces balls."

"You're right." Mr. Bobbsey smiled. "And we'll be sure to take some balls along and try it."

The rest of the day the twins could talk of little else besides the trip. Mrs. Bobbsey, with Nan's and Dinah's help, started making a list of articles they would take with them.

During the next two weeks the twins visited the houseboat every day after school and twice on Saturday and Sunday. And what a flurry of shopping and packing there was in the Bobbsey household!

Dinah groaned a bit about what she was sure would be a rough voyage, but finally she agreed to go.

"I'll ask Daddy to stay close to shore," Flossie told her. "Then you won't feel seasick."

The cook had to grin at this. "Well, honey child," she said, "I won't worry any more."

Two days before they were to leave, Bert walked over to the lake to see if the carpenters and painters had finished work on the houseboat. While he was watching from the dock, Danny Rugg suddenly came up.

"I'm going on board," he announced.

"Oh, no, you're not," Bert said. "My father gave orders for everyone to stay off until the workmen are through."

"Think you're pretty good, don't you?" said Danny with a sneer. "Nobody's going to keep me off."

"Listen, Danny," Bert began. But before he could finish his sentence, the other boy gave Bert a hard shove and he fell backwards off the dock into the lake.

Bert was furious. He swam quickly to the surface, choking a little from his unexpected dousing. He lost no time in getting to shore. Paying no attention to his dripping clothes, he angrily faced the bully.

Danny retreated a few steps—but not in time. Bert hit him with a flying tackle and both boys fell to the ground. Although Danny was heavier, Bert was much quicker and soon he was getting the better of his opponent.

"This'll teach you to start a fight," he said, sitting firmly on Danny's chest and holding the boy's shoulders to the ground.

"Okay, okay," Danny gasped, squirming. "Let me up!"

Bert did this, but did not relax his guard until Danny admitted he had had enough and walked sullenly away. He paused long enough to point a finger at the houseboat and call back threateningly to Bert:

"You'll be sorry you didn't let my dad buy the boat. Just wait!"

He ran off and Bert started for home. Once there, he went to his room and changed into dry clothes. Bert decided not to say anything about his meeting with Danny. No sense in worrying his family two days before the start of the trip, he thought.

Later that evening, as Flossie and Freddie were saying good night to the others in the living room, the telephone rang.

"I'll answer it," said Mr. Bobbsey. He walked over and picked up the phone. "Hello?" Then he exclaimed, "What! Yes, I'll be there right away. I wonder how it happened."

"What's the matter?" cried Mrs. Bobbsey in alarm as he hung up.

"The call was from the lake police patrol," Mr. Bobbsey said. "The *Bluebird* has been found adrift on the lake!"

CHAPTER III

A TOY CHRISTENING

THE BOBBSEYS were stunned. What had caused their houseboat to go adrift? Was it damaged so they could not go on the trip?

Mr. Bobbsey was already outdoors, hurrying to his car when Bert said, "Mother, I'd like to go with Dad."

"And I want to," cried Nan.

"All right," Mrs. Bobbsey consented, and the twins quickly put on sweaters and raced to the driveway. Their father was backing out the small car he used for business.

"Mind if we come?" Nan asked. "Maybe we can help!"

"Hop in!" said Mr. Bobbsey. As they drove off, he added, "I wonder how our boat got loose."

"Maybe the ropes were cut by rubbing against the dock," Nan suggested. "There's enough breeze tonight to do it."

"Perhaps you're right," said her father. "Too bad we hadn't dropped anchor. I'll get one of our small tugs from the lumberyard and go across the lake."

A half hour later, the three Bobbseys arrived at the opposite side of Lake Metoka in the tug. Three officers of the lake police patrol were waiting for them on board the *Bluebird*. A muscular-looking man with a sunburned face stepped forward as the twins and their father walked the plank laid from the tug to the houseboat.

"Hello, Chief Mahoney," Mr. Bobbsey greeted the patrol captain and introduced the children. "Is there much damage aboard?"

"I don't think so," the officer answered, "but maybe you'd better look around yourself. One of my men found your houseboat when he was patrolling the lake. Good thing he did before she could snarl up water traffic."

"I'm sorry this happened," Mr. Bobbsey said, as Bert and Nan hurried off to examine the boat. "I recently bought the *Bluebird* and repairs were being made on the boat, but I'm certain she was tied up securely."

Meanwhile, Bert and Nan had found everything all right in the cabin. Now they hurried to look at the sleeping quarters, galley, and hold. There was no damage. Relieved they returned to their father and the police. Mr. Bobbsey was pleased to learn that these sections of the houseboat were intact.

"I guess everything's okay," he declared finally. "We're lucky."

"We sure are," Bert said. "But I'd like to know how the *Bluebird* got loose."

Chief Mahoney suggested that Mr. Bobbsey examine the rope which had held the boat to the dock. One end was attached to a cleat at the bow. The other end, however, was frayed and ragged.

"Do you think it was caused by rubbing against the dock?" Bert asked, and then before Chief Mahoney could answer, the boy exclaimed, "Sir! I think this rope has been cut!"

"I think you're right," said the officer. "And I wonder if this might belong to the culprit." He held up a tan, peaked cap. "Do you recognize it?"

Bert gave a gasp. "Why that's—" He stopped suddenly. The cap looked exactly like the one Danny Rugg had been wearing that afternoon!

"Do you know to whom it belongs?" Mr. Bobbsey prompted as he and Chief Mahoney looked at Bert expectantly.

"I—ah—I thought so at first, Dad. But I could be mistaken." Bert thought it best not to accuse Danny unless he had positive proof.

Chief Mahoney now said, "We'll have your houseboat towed back to the dock and drop anchor. You folks planning to use her soon?"

"We're going on a trip day after tomorrow," Bert spoke up, and his father added, "We don't want anything to happen which will postpone our departure."

"Then we'll keep an eye on her for the next two nights," Captain Mahoney promised. "Just in case someone tries to set her loose again."

"That's very kind of you," thanked Mr. Bobbsey. "I'm sorry to have caused you so much trouble."

As the twins and their father went back on board the tug, Captain Mahoney called, "If you find out who owns that cap, let me know."

Bert now decided to confide in Mr. Bobbsey and Nan. He told them his suspicions about the cap and of his tussle with Danny that afternoon.

"I'm sure Danny set our boat adrift," Bert said. "He warned we'd be sorry we didn't let his father buy the boat."

"Well, the Lake Patrol will guard against any more tricks," Mr. Bobbsey assured his son. "But you were right not to say anything about the cap. You can't accuse Danny without proof."

When they reached home, Mrs. Bobbsey listened intently to the story, then said, "Fortunately no harm was done. And now, off to bed. Remember, your cousins are arriving tomorrow!"

Permission had been granted by Dorothy's and Harry's parents for the two children to join the Lakeport Bobbseys. Since both the twins' mother and father would be busy all the next morning, the children were going to meet the visitors alone. Freddie had offered to take along his wagon to carry back their suitcases.

Early the following day the twins hurried to the railroad station to greet the visitors. Dorothy had been spending a few days at Meadow Brook, so the cousins were arriving together.

"Oh, I'm so glad you could come!" cried Nan a few minutes later as Dorothy climbed down the steps of the train and flung her arms around Nan's neck.

"I can hardly wait for the boat trip!" exclaimed Dorothy, her violet-blue eyes dancing. Though she was a tomboy at times and wore her dark hair short, she was a very pretty girl. She hugged Flossie as if she had not seen her in years.

"Hi, Harry!" yelled Bert and Freddie, and rushed to greet their cousin as he stepped onto the platform. Though Harry was Bert's age, he was a good bit huskier, probably because of all the outdoor work he did on the farm. The blond, suntanned boy grinned happily, said hello to Nan, and tweaked Flossie's curls.

"Ship ahoy!" he shouted. "When do we see the battle cruiser?"

"Oh, it's a nice, peaceful home boat," Flossie said quickly. "But there's lots of room for all of us."

"How are Snap and Snoop?" asked Harry.

"Okay. They're going with us on the trip," said Bert.

"Snap's mad," Freddie announced. "We haven't taken him aboard yet, but we will to-day."

"'Cause there's a surprise!" added Flossie. "And you're just in time for it!" She looked at Dorothy and Harry with a mysterious expression. They tried to guess what this might be, but the little girl shook her blond head. "You have to wait," she said firmly.

Bert and Nan looked at their small sister questioningly. They had not heard of any surprise. But Freddie apparently had, for he began to giggle. "It's a nifty surprise," he said.

The visiting cousins were brought up to date on all that had happened recently. Then, directly after lunch, Mr. Bobbsey announced that the *Bluebird* was back at the dock and that all work aboard had been completed.

"We'll drive down now and get organized," he said. "Then we'll be ready to set sail tomorrow."

As they started out in the large family car, Freddie carried his new sailboat under one arm and Flossie was clutching a small paper bag. She refused to tell what was in it. Snap and Snoop were in the rear on Bert's and Nan's laps.

In a few minutes they came in sight of the *Bluebird*.

"Oh!" Dorothy and Harry exclaimed.

How attractive and cheerful the houseboat looked in the bright sunshine, with her fresh coat of white paint and deep pink shutters on the little windows! Gay chintz curtains helped to create a festive air.

"Now we're going to have the surprise," Flossie announced as the group filed out of the car.

She led them to the water. As they stood wondering, Freddie placed his sailboat on the edge of the bank. He turned it so the others could see a name painted on it.

DUCK-A-WAY

"How cute!" said Dorothy. "Who thought of that?"

"Freddie did," Flossie answered proudly. "And we're going to christen the boat." She opened the bag and brought out a little bottle of ginger ale. "Ready, Freddie?"

"Get set!" he cried, setting the boat in the water and holding onto it. "Go!"

With this Flossie banged the bottle hard on

the bow of the toy sailboat and said solemnly, "I name you *Duck-A-Way!*"

Freddie let go of the boat. It wobbled a moment in the water, caught the breeze, and scooted down the lake shore. Freddie ran after it and in a few moments reached out and grasped his toy. The others clapped and Mr. Bobbsey said, "Hurrah for the *Duck-A-Way!* May she have good sailing!"

Then everyone went aboard the houseboat. After the cousins had seen the cabin, Nan said, "Come on, Dorothy. I want to show you the bedroom we'll share with Flossie. There are three bunks and you may have first choice."

Bert and Freddie led Harry to the sleeping cabin they had selected.

"This is terrific!" Harry said with enthusiasm, looking around the pine-paneled room. "I'm glad I brought my short-wave set along. Did you fellows know that I have my license as a 'ham' radio operator?"

"Wonderful!" Bert exclaimed. "Maybe you can teach me something about it."

"I like ham, too!" said Freddie.

Harry explained to Freddie that a "ham" radio operator did not mean food, but a person who could get radio messages from all over the country—and even outside the country. Then the three boys joined Mr. and Mrs. Bobbsey and the girls in the main cabin.

"I'd like to be Communications Officer on this boat, Uncle Richard," said Harry, and explained about his short-wave set. "In charge of all ship-to-shore communications," he added.

"Of course!" Mr. Bobbsey replied. "We'll all have titles just like in the Navy. But in the Navy they call them ratings."

"And everyone will be responsible for certain duties!" Mrs. Bobbsey said.

"I'll be the fire fighter," said Freddie at once.

"I'll be head of the toys," Flossie said.

Bert grinned. "And put every one of them away at night," he teased.

Further planning was interrupted by the sound of someone walking on the deck. Mr. Bobbsey looked at the group and counted noses.

"Everyone's here!" he announced.

Then who was on the deck? Was it Danny Rugg, trying to add more mischief to what he had already done? The children looked at one another with questioning eyes.

Whoever was on deck had not been invited!

CHAPTER IV

THE CAPTAIN

"WE'D better see who's on deck!" Bert urged.

By this time Snap was barking furiously outside the cabin. When the Bobbseys stepped through the doorway, they saw the dog standing guard over a boy about ten years old dressed in jeans and a large straw hat. He crouched in fright against the deck railing.

"Quiet, Snap!" Bert ordered. "It's all right."

Snap looked at his young master with a puzzled expression, but obediently stopped barking and sat down in front of the strange boy.

"I didn't take anything! Honest I didn't!" exclaimed the lad, standing up slowly. "I was just looking at your boat."

"That's perfectly all right," Mr. Bobbsey said kindly.

Mrs. Bobbsey gazed with pity at the threadbare blue jeans and ragged shirt the boy was wearing. His thin body and pale face made her realize he was undernourished.

Flossie, who always liked to meet new people, walked over to the boy and asked, "What's your name?"

"Bruce Watson," the lad replied, glancing down at the deck shyly.

"Welcome aboard, Bruce," said Mr. Bobbsey, trying to put the caller at ease. "Perhaps you'd like to inspect the *Bluebird.*"

"Sure he would!" agreed Freddie. "I'll be his guide."

For a moment Bruce's face brightened, but then he said, "No, I—I guess I'd better not. I have to be getting home. Thanks anyway."

"Where is your home?" asked Nan, sensing that the boy was not happy and wishing she could help him.

"I live on a farm on Lemby Creek, up at the end of Lake Metoka," Bruce replied. "I came down to Lakeport on an errand."

He was about to say more when a commotion at the end of the gangplank interrupted them. Dinah and Sam, her husband, who drove one of Mr. Bobbsey's lumber trucks, were trudging up. Their arms were laden with baskets of supplies which they had brought in the truck.

As the cook started to step onto the deck, a streak of black fur went past directly in front of her.

"Land's sakes!" Dinah exclaimed. "Now a black cat's crossed my path! This trip's sure enough goin' to bring bad luck to Dinah!"

"This isn't just any old black cat, Dinah!" Flossie objected. "This is our Snoop." The little girl leaned over and picked up the plump cat, stroking his white chest.

"Did you bring some cookies and milk with you, Dinah?" asked Freddie, patting her on the arm.

Dinah looked at the chubby little boy and suddenly laughed. "It's the same on a houseboat as it is at home," she said. "Show me where the kitchen is, Freddie, and I'll give you enough for everybody."

As the two went inside, Bert turned to Bruce again. "How did you get here?" he asked.

"I hitchhiked most of the way and walked the rest."

"That must be over twenty miles!" exclaimed Harry, remembering the location of Lemby Creek on a map he had been studying.

"It's twenty-one, to be exact," Bruce replied, warming up to the other children.

Freddie reappeared and offered him one of Dinah's homemade cookies. Bruce hungrily took a large bite out of it and Freddie urged him to have more.

"You should have asked your mother to drive you over," said Flossie, putting Snoop on the railing of the boat. The cat did not seem to like it there and jumped off, running down the deck to the stern of the boat.

"My mother died several years ago," Bruce replied. "I live with my stepfather, Mr. Hardman. He sent me on an errand in Lakeport and said I should get there the best way I could. I was lucky and two nice people gave me short rides. The last one dropped me here, and I saw your boat."

"I know Mr. Hardman," Bert's father spoke up. "And I met your mother once, a long time ago. She was a lovely woman, Bruce. You look a lot like her."

Bruce smiled for the first time that afternoon. "Yes, Mother was wonderful!" he said. "Mr. Hardman used to be nice, too," he went on. "But ever since Mother died, he's been grouchy as an old bear. He's mean, too. Sometimes he beats—" Bruce stopped speaking suddenly, looking as if he had said too much.

"Beats what?" asked Mrs. Bobbsey, who was eager to learn the rest of the boy's story.

"Beats me at games," said Bruce, leaning down to pat Snap, who was now licking his hand. But the others felt he had meant to tell something else.

Just then Sam came out on deck. "I'm going back soon, Mr. Bobbsey," he announced. "Anything else you want me to do?"

"Wait a few minutes, Sam," Mr. Bobbsey replied. "Then take Bruce with you. After he does his errand in Lakeport, you can run him over to his farm. It's pretty far for him to walk back to the highway."

The boy flashed Mr. Bobbsey a grateful look. Freddie took hold of his arm and said he would show him the boat before he left.

"You're lucky folks," Bruce said wistfully, peeking into the cabins. "I've never had a vacation. At least, not for a long time. I remember once playing on a nice sandy beach. There were palm trees and some pretty houses."

"When was that?" Nan asked him.

But Bruce was looking dreamily away into the distance and did not seem to hear her. "There was a boat, too, but I don't know what kind." The lad smiled at his companions. "Maybe I just dreamed it all or saw it in a movie."

He followed Freddie and the other boys around on a tour of the *Bluebird,* admiring everything. When the boys returned to the main deck, Bruce thanked Mr. and Mrs. Bobbsey and the children for being so nice to him.

"Sam is ready to go, Bruce," Bert said. "I'll walk to the truck with you."

Flossie came running over as they stepped onto the gangplank. "Here!" she cried, handing Bruce a large bag of cookies. "Freddie and I thought you might get hungry on the way home. We always do."

"Thank you," Bruce said, smiling at the little girl and waving good-by to everyone.

As he and Bert walked to the truck, Bruce said, "If I could have friends like you folks, I wouldn't want to run away so much."

"Run away?" repeated Bert.

"Yes, to try to find my uncle—my mother's brother. I think he lives somewhere in the South. I've gone through all Mom's papers, but I can't find his address. And he hasn't written to me since she's been gone."

"That's a shame," said Bert. "What's his name?"

"I—I can't remember his other name. Just John. I hope I'll hear from him because I can't stand living where I am much longer," Bruce said with a sigh.

"Maybe my dad can help you when we get back," Bert suggested.

"Thanks. I'll try to stick it out that long," Bruce said with a smile, as they reached the truck. He hopped inside next to Sam. "See you in about a month!"

As the truck rolled down the road, Bert walked back to the *Bluebird*. He was deep in thought, wondering about Bruce Watson's life.

"Hey, Bert!" shouted Freddie, running toward his brother. "Don't go back to the boat. We're going home now. Daddy has some business to take care of this afternoon!"

The Bobbseys returned to their rambling, old-fashioned house with Harry and Dorothy. They started gathering toys and games for the trip. Flossie asked her mother for her allowance, saying she had some last-minute shopping to do. Nan promised to join her sister as she wanted to drop off some books at the library.

When the girls returned a little later, Flossie proudly showed a tiny white raincoat and boots for her doll, Betty Lou, to Dinah.

"Mighty fancy," the cook commented.

Nan said with a laugh, "Flossie bought them to keep her doll from getting wet when the waves go over the side of our boat."

"Waves!" Dinah exclaimed. "Oh dear me, now I know I'll get seasick."

"Oh, Flossie's only pretending," said Nan, and Dinah felt better.

The front door opened and Mr. Bobbsey called out, "Anybody home? We have company!"

The children and their mother and cousins hurried to the living room. Standing there with Mr. Bobbsey was the tallest man they had ever seen outside of a circus. He was about six feet four inches in height and wore a bristly red beard. He had a square-jawed face, which was burned a deep reddish brown. But his deep blue eyes were friendly and smiling.

"This is Captain Frank McGinty," said Mr. Bobbsey and introduced the members of his family. "He used to run the *Bluebird* for Mr. Enslow."

"Ahoy, mates!" boomed the captain in a voice which reminded the children of a foghorn. Flossie and Freddie jumped.

"Captain McGinty is going to run the *Bluebird* for us," added Mr. Bobbsey. "I told him we were talking about ratings and duties on board. He's going to stay to supper and help us assign them."

"Goody!" exclaimed Freddie and Flossie together, as Mrs. Bobbsey invited the guests to sit down.

"This is Captain Frank McGinty"

"Everyone will have a job!" the captain announced in a strong, decisive voice.

"I'd like to be the radio operator!" said Harry instantly.

Captain McGinty pulled on his beard and looked at Harry. "What are your qualifications?" he asked. When Harry told him he was a ham operator, the officer said, "All right."

The captain now turned to the rest of the group. Then he pulled a paper and pencil from his green and black flannel shirt and began to write.

The Bobbseys waited. Finally the captain stood up, put the pencil back into his pocket and said, "Attention!" in such a stern voice that everyone else stood up. "I shall now read my list of officers!" he announced.

"Mr. Bobbsey—Engineer.
Mrs. Bobbsey—Quartermaster.
Bert Bobbsey—First Mate.
Nan and Dorothy—Second and Third Mates.
Harry—Communications Officer.
Dinah—Chief Cook.

Flossie and Freddie looked at each other. They were almost in tears. Everyone but themselves had a job!

"You speak to him, Freddie!" urged Flossie, pushing her twin forward. "He forgot us!"

The little boy looked up at the tall captain,

who was talking to Bert in an unusually low voice. He paid no attention to Freddie. Finally Freddie could stand it no longer.

"What's the rate for Flossie and me?" he asked in a loud voice.

Captain McGinty looked down at him and said, "You're my crew. Seamen! Swabbies! You'll clean the decks."

Flossie and Freddie were too scared to object, but they did not feel as though they would like such a job.

"There'll be a chance for a promotion if you do your work well," the officer added.

"I'm going out and tell Dinah!" exclaimed Freddie to his twin. "She'll help us out."

He ran pell-mell through the hall and into the dining room which the cook was just entering. She carried a large cake with pink icing on it.

"Good land of mercy!" yelled Dinah as Freddie bumped into her. "Wha—wha—"

But that was all she could say. Dinah tried to save herself from falling, but could not. Neither could Freddie, and both sat down hard.

The cake flew from Dinah's hands up toward her head, turned over, then fell into her lap.

CHAPTER V

THE "BLUEBIRD" SAILS

FREDDIE was frightened. The cake was ruined and Dinah looked very unhappy.

"Did—did I hurt you, Dinah?" he asked. "I'm sorry I knocked you down."

"I'm kind of shook up," the cook replied, picking herself up with a groan. "But I'll be all right. How do you feel, Freddie?"

"Okay. But there won't be any dessert tonight."

"Now don't you worry, honey child," said Dinah. "I'll fix up something else in a jiffy. But why were you runnin' so fast?"

"To tell you about Flossie and me. We have to scrub the deck!"

Dinah laughed heartily and said, "Oh, you'll have plenty of time to play, too."

This made Freddie feel better and he ate two helpings of everything at supper, even the applesauce fluff dessert. During the meal Captain McGinty told of his adventures at sea.

The children liked best the one about the

parrot on board a sailing vessel, who did not like the cook's cat and disappeared. Three days later, when everyone was sure the bird was lost on the ocean, a sailor found it in the crow's nest having a chat with a sea gull.

When supper was over and the captain was ready to leave, he said, "Well, my hearties, I'm an old sea dog who likes to keep everything shipshape and on time. We'll shove off promptly at ten-thirty tomorrow morning. I'll expect my officers and crew earlier, though." He then thanked Mrs. Bobbsey for the meal and with a brisk "Good night, everyone," strode off.

"Whew!" said Dorothy with a giggle. "We'd better be on time!"

The following morning everyone was busy with last-minute packing. Mrs. Bobbsey caught Flossie trying to pack eight dolls into hers!

"Only two," her mother advised, so Flossie decided on Betty Lou, and a doll named Cuddles.

"Oh dear," sighed the little girl, "and I promised them all they could sleep on the houseboat."

Mrs. Bobbsey suggested that the others could have a turn later.

"Goody," said Flossie. "Then we can take another trip."

An hour before departure time, Nan, Bert, Harry, and Dorothy went into town on a mysterious errand. They promised to meet the others at the *Bluebird*.

"Don't be late," Mr. Bobbsey called, "or the captain will sail without you!"

"We sure won't," Bert assured him.

Sam loaded one of the lumber trucks with suitcases, boxes, and the rest of the supplies. When he was ready to go, Flossie, Freddie, and Dinah climbed into the back of the truck. Mr. and Mrs. Bobbsey got into the cab with Sam.

As the truck rumbled down the street, Flossie exclaimed, "We forgot Snoop and Snap! Tell Sam to turn around!"

Dinah grinned. "They're already aboard. Sam took them down to the boat early."

"Oh!" said Flossie, ashamed because she had almost overlooked their pets.

As Sam pulled the truck alongside the *Bluebird,* the small twins saw Captain McGinty standing at the gangplank. There was a frown on his face as he paced up and down the dock, frequently looking at his wrist watch.

"My officers and crew are late!" he said sternly when the group came forward. "This ship departs promptly at ten-thirty."

"Sorry, Captain," Mr. Bobbsey said cheerfully. "It's always a job closing up the house."

"Well, I'll overlook it this time, but don't let it happen again!" Then the captain commanded, "Announce yourselves!"

Mr. and Mrs. Bobbsey walked aboard, giving their titles of Engineer and Quartermaster.

"Chief Cook, sir!" said Dinah in a deep voice, as she stepped on deck.

"Yes?" roared the captain, looking at Flossie and Freddie, who were timidly following behind Dinah.

"Seaman," Flossie said with a smile, for she had decided to like the captain.

"Swabbie!" piped Freddie, who was not quite able to look the officer in the eye.

"Welcome aboard!" Captain McGinty boomed, and shook their hands. Unexpectedly he looked down at the little twins and gave them a friendly grin.

"I'll do all I can to help," Freddie said in a meek voice.

"Sure you will!" the officer nodded. Then he picked up a pair of binoculars and scanned the wooded area near the shoreline.

"Where are the First, Second, and Third Mates and the Communications Officer?" the captain demanded to know.

"They went into town," Mrs. Bobbsey said. "I expect they'll be here in a few minutes."

"I hope so," said Captain McGinty. "At ten-thirty sharp we pull up the anchor! In the meantime," he continued, "the seamen will hoist the flag!"

Flossie and Freddie, who were anxiously

peering up the road for the other children, looked up at the captain. "What flag?" Freddie inquired.

In reply, the officer reached into a pocket of his navy blue jacket and pulled out a neatly folded American flag.

"This will be your job each day, Seaman Freddie," he said. "Promptly at eight in the morning you will hoist the flag on yonder pole! The minute the sun starts to go down, you will lower the flag, Seaman Flossie."

"I'll be glad to," said Freddie. "As long as it doesn't keep me from breakfast."

"Nothing must interfere with flag detail!" Captain McGinty said firmly.

He then showed Freddie how to attach the flag to the ropes of the pole and pull it up until the flag reached the top. Flossie and her parents watched with great interest.

"Fine," said the captain. He looked at his watch. "Hm-mm, 10:28. Well, I'll pull up anchor in two minutes."

"Oh, but we have to wait for Bert and Nan!" Flossie cried anxiously.

"And Harry and Dorothy," added Freddie.

"Nobody can hold up sailing time," declared Captain McGinty.

Flossie and Freddie were fearful as he seemed about to untie the mooring ropes. Suddenly Freddie interrupted him with a happy scream. "Wait! Wait! Here they come!"

Flossie ran down the gangplank, waving her arms wildly to the other children. They were running as fast as they could. Each boy was carrying a large package and the girls had smaller ones.

"We're leaving in two minutes!" screamed Flossie. "Hurry!"

Snap saw the children, too, and ran across the gangplank, barking happily. The late arrivals rushed on deck out of breath.

"Sorry, Dad," Bert explained. "Our errand took longer than we thought."

By now Sam had all the baggage and supplies on the houseboat and was saying good-by to everyone. How sorry the children were that he was not going on the trip with them! But Mr. Bobbsey had asked Sam to remain in Lakeport and look after the house.

Captain McGinty ordered the boys to untie the houseboat, then said, "Pull up the anchor."

A few minutes later, Bert and Harry had the anchor on board. "We're ready, Captain," Harry announced.

The twins watched the shoreline of Lakeport recede until the *Bluebird* moved out of sight of it around a bend in the lake. Then Nan and Dorothy went to their cabin to unpack and admire each other's clothes. Harry went into the cabin he was sharing with Bert and

Freddie and set up his little short-wave radio.

"What are you doing, Harry?" asked Bert, coming to the cabin a few minutes later.

His cousin was standing on a stool in front of the doorway. He had a hammer and some nails in his hand.

"I'm going to put this up," Harry replied. He held out a sign which read: *Communications Shack.*

"Want any help?" asked Bert.

"No, thanks," Harry replied. "I'm almost through."

"Then I'm going to get out some of the maps and charts," said Bert. "Dad suggested that we put them on the wall in the main cabin."

"Good idea," Harry nodded approvingly.

In the meantime, Mrs. Bobbsey and Flossie had gone to the galley to see how Dinah was getting along. Although the place was untidy with many packages and boxes of food, Dinah was efficiently putting things away.

"See what I have here," she said, holding out a large brown bottle.

"What is it, Dinah?" asked Mrs. Bobbsey.

"Seasick pills!" the cook announced, rolling her eyes. "You wouldn't catch old Dinah without 'em. I'm goin' to take some as soon as this boat leaves the dock."

Flossie looked at her mother and started to giggle. The boat had left the dock fifteen minutes before! Evidently Dinah had been so busy that she had not noticed when they set off.

"What's the matter?" asked Dinah, gazing at Flossie suspiciously.

The little girl pointed to the window. Dinah rushed over and looked out. "Goodness me!" she cried. "Where's the land? Oh, I feel sick!"

Mrs. Bobbsey smiled. "That just proves it's only your imagination, Dinah."

"I guess so," Dinah admitted, chuckling, and went back to her work.

At this moment the captain's voice rang out, *"All hands on deck!"*

The three hurried outside and looked up at the wheelhouse of the *Bluebird* where the captain stood very straight. The others arrived one by one. A giggle came from the twins as they saw their father appear with black, sooty face and hands.

"The engine is in good order!" he said triumphantly.

"But you're not, Richard," laughed his wife. "Better wash before you report to the captain!"

"I'd like the Engineer to wait for just one moment," Captain McGinty said. "Will the First Mate and Communications Officer open their packages, please!" he added.

Freddie and Flossie could hardly wait. What was inside the mysterious bundles?

CHAPTER VI

CAT OVERBOARD!

BERT and Harry tore the paper off the big packages they had carried on board the houseboat.

Flossie and Freddie stood as close as they could to the boys so they would be the first to see the contents. Even Mr. and Mrs. Bobbsey were eager to learn what was inside.

"Oh, look!" cried Freddie happily, as Bert finished unwrapping his package. "Caps!"

"Yachting caps for the officers," said Harry. "And sailor caps for Flossie and Freddie." He picked up one and perched it on Freddie's hair.

"See what Nan and I have," said Dorothy, showing the others some imitation insignia they had purchased.

"Ahem!" Captain McGinty cleared his throat. The twins looked around and he was smiling broadly. "The Second and Third Mates will sew the insignia on each cap," he ordered.

"What's insignia?" asked Flossie.

"Badges with pictures on to tell the kind of work you do in the Navy, Flossie," Captain McGinty explained. "Naval officers have theirs sewed on their coats, but Nan and Dorothy will put yours on your caps instead."

"But we don't get any," Freddie said, " 'cause we're only crew."

"But ours are different and I like mine better," Flossie declared.

Her twin decided he did, too, and said, "I hope I don't lose my cap. No one will know who I am!"

"The caps were Captain McGinty's idea," Bert said, handing a high chef's hat to Dinah.

"And it was his treat, too!" Nan added. "Wasn't that nice of him?"

Mr. and Mrs. Bobbsey and the children thanked the officer and he turned away, looking very embarrassed.

"It was nothing!" he muttered gruffly. "And now the Quartermaster will show you where the life preservers are and help you adjust them."

Mrs. Bobbsey led the group to a locker which stood against the cabin and opened it. She took out a life jacket, slipped her arms through the straps and buckled it. The others did the same, and after a few tries even Flossie and Freddie could adjust them easily.

"Oh, my goodness, something's burning!" cried Dinah and dashed off.

Near lunchtime the children heard a loud din in the corridor and hurried to see what it was. They stopped short and laughed loudly. Dinah was banging on a dishpan to call everyone to lunch.

After a hearty lunch, the three boys got out the fish poles and tackle and dangled their lines from the side of the boat in the water. A gentle breeze barely ruffled the surface of the lake. In a little while Mr. Bobbsey walked over to where they were leaning on the rail and said, "No bites yet?"

"We've had two or three nibbles," Bert answered hopefully.

"You'll probably have better luck when we reach a quiet place and anchor," Mr. Bobbsey said.

"I'm going to catch more fish than anyone!" Freddie boasted. "And I'm going to save them and put them in a fish bowl."

"Good idea, son," said Mr. Bobbsey. "But in that case, you'd better just catch little fish."

"It will be a big bowl," insisted Freddie. "I think I'll look for one right now."

The small boy placed his pole on the deck and ran to the galley. In a few moments a dull thud came from that part of the boat.

"What was that?" cried Mrs. Bobbsey, who

was in the main cabin helping the girls sew on the insignia.

"Look what you've done, Freddie!" they heard Dinah exclaim, and hurried to the galley.

Flossie was the first to reach it. "Ha! Ha!" she laughed loudly. "Look at Freddie's new hat!"

What a strange picture Freddie made! He was standing on one of the counters with a red flowerpot perched on top of his head. The floor was coated white with flour and salt.

There was an expression of dismay on Freddie's face as he tugged at the flowerpot. The others realized it would not budge.

"I was looking for a fish bowl," the little boy explained hastily. "I tried this on for size and it got stuck."

"And look at my floor that was spic-span clean!" Dinah wailed.

In the little boy's haste, he had knocked over a tin of flour and a container of salt. As Mrs. Bobbsey helped her son to the floor and gently pulled the flowerpot off the top of his head, Nan and Dorothy grabbed a broom and a mop to sweep the floor.

"Thank you," Dinah said gratefully. She grinned at Freddie. "I sure am glad you won't have to wear that flowerpot on your head for the rest of your life!"

Just then Mr. Bobbsey called from on deck, "I think Bert has a bite on his line. Come and see!"

"Let's go!" shouted Freddie, almost knocking Flossie over in his haste to see the first fish caught. Mrs. Bobbsey, Nan, and Dorothy hurried after the young twins. When they reached the deck, Bert was reeling in the taut line.

"Easy!" Mr. Bobbsey cautioned, as he and Harry supervised.

Bert, in his eagerness, gave the line a quick jerk. Something flashed in the sunlight and the next moment a small fish flopped on the deck, right in front of where Snoop was sleeping.

"Oh!" cried Bert in disappointment, looking at his catch. "It's only a little sunfish!"

Snoop awakened with a jump and when he spied the flopping fish, made a leap for it. But the fish was wet and slippery and as Snoop pounced on it, the fish slid across the deck toward the railing.

"I want that for my collection!" Freddie exclaimed, running forward.

But Snoop was quicker than Freddie and gave another leap toward the sunfish. But before he reached it, the fish slid off the deck into the water. Snoop was so intent on catching the slippery creature that he, too, went under the railing and fell into the lake.

"Cat overboard!" cried Captain McGinty,

who had been watching from the wheelhouse
for the past few minutes. He shut off the engine
and the *Bluebird* shuddered to a halt.

Snap gave a loud bark and tried to get under the railing. He was too large, so he jumped
up to the rail and leaped overboard.

"Snap's up to his old tricks," said Nan with
a smile. "He's going to see that his cat friend
doesn't come to any harm."

"Dog overboard!" yelled Mr. Bobbsey and
rushed toward a deck locker from which he
pulled a fishnet.

By this time Snap had swum to where poor
Snoop was paddling about in the water. The
brave dog gently took hold of the loose fur at
the back of Snoop's neck. Then, holding the
cat's head well up out of the water, Snap
started back for the *Bluebird*.

"I wish he'd caught the sunfish too," said
Freddie wistfully.

"You can catch another," said Nan, then
asked, "How are we going to get Snap and
Snoop back on board?"

The Bobbseys looked down at the distance
between the deck and the water line. It was
about six feet. Obviously, no one could reach
down far enough to lift up the two animals.
And the iron ladder was on the other side of
the houseboat.

Suddenly Bert had an idea. He began to discard his outer clothing. In a moment he dived into the water.

"Attaboy, Bert!" Harry yelled.

"Be careful, Bert," his mother advised. "Don't let Snoop scratch you!"

Bert grinned and waved to the group on deck. In no time he reached the animals and, turning, swam alongside Snap as they made their way back to the houseboat.

"I'll try to lift Snap and Snoop out of the water," Bert called up. "You take them."

Hearing this, Mr. Bobbsey climbed over the rail, held on with one hand and reached down with his other. Bert was able to lift Snap high enough out of the water so that his father could grab Snoop. Once he had the cat on deck, he reached down for Snap.

The two animals shook the water off their fur and Snoop, thoroughly disgusted, headed for a sunny spot to lick himself and dry out. Snap stood next to the children, barking at Bert gratefully.

"Good work, Bert!" Mr. Bobbsey congratulated his son. "Your turn now to come aboard."

"I think I'll take a little swim first," Bert announced.

"Better not, pal," Harry called. "I think Cap McGinty wants to get started."

"I'll just take a quickie," Bert said, swimming about fifty feet away from the *Bluebird*. Turning around, he yelled, "Water's fine. Why don't you all come in?"

"There isn't that much time," Harry called back.

Mr. Bobbsey was about to tell Bert to return to the houseboat when the captain picked up a megaphone and roared:

"Come aboard, First Mate, or you'll be confined to quarters!"

Bert quickly swam back to the iron ladder on the other side of the houseboat and climbed up.

Scarcely had the swimmer's feet touched the deck when Captain McGinty's voice boomed, "Bert Bobbsey, come to my quarters at once!"

CHAPTER VII

NAN'S MISHAP

"I'M IN TROUBLE, I guess!" Bert exclaimed, looking at his father and Harry for support.

"Better go see the captain right away," Mr. Bobbsey urged, with an expressionless face.

"Alone?" asked Bert, hoping that someone would volunteer to go with him.

"Certainly!" Mr. Bobbsey said, as if there were no other choice.

Bert climbed unhappily up to the wheelhouse and paused. He knew he had been wrong in holding up the *Bluebird*'s trip just to take a swim. To himself, he said:

"All right, Bert. You had your fun. Now take the consequences."

Before the boy had time to open the door, Captain McGinty did so. "Come in, First Mate," he said in a stern voice.

In the meantime Harry had gathered the other children together. "It doesn't seem right to punish Bert after he made the rescue," he protested.

"No, it doesn't," agreed Nan.

"Let's hide outside the wheelhouse and listen," said Harry. "And if Bert needs help, we'll go in."

Quietly they all tiptoed up. Inside the wheelhouse the officer stared at the boy several seconds before speaking.

"In the Navy everyone works for the good of the ship," he said very seriously.

"Yes, sir," Bert agreed.

"Men always obey orders," the captain went on.

"I know," said Bert.

The officer walked over to the door and suddenly yanked it open. Five children tumbled in through the open doorway.

"Eavesdroppers!" roared the captain.

The children shamefacedly got to their feet and apologized.

"It was my fault," said Harry. "I—"

"Silence!"

Freddie and Flossie began to tremble. What would this stern man do to them?

"Every ship has rules and regulations," the officer continued. "One of the rules on the *Bluebird* is that nobody is to go swimming without permission. You must swim in pairs, because there is always a chance that one person may get a cramp or have some other trouble while swimming."

"I'm sorry, sir," Bert said. "I didn't know about the rule."

"It is posted on a list in the main cabin. I suggest that you all go and read the rules immediately," McGinty said. "And I'll add another. No more eavesdropping!"

"We promise," the children said in chorus. Then, as they started to leave, he roared, "I haven't dismissed you yet!"

He crossed the little room and yanked open a drawer of an old chest. "Here, mates, have some candy!" he offered, holding out a box of chocolate bars.

As they hesitated, the officer said, "I'm not angry at any of you children. But rules are rules on board ship." After each child had taken a candy bar, he added, "When we anchor in shallow water later this afternoon, everyone can have a swim. Officers and crew dismissed!"

As they climbed down to the deck, the children heard the engine start and soon the *Bluebird* was under way again. Half an hour later the captain dropped anchor in a cove near a pleasant little grove of trees.

"We'll spend the night here," he announced. "And there's good swimming."

The children and grownups too put on swim suits and soon were in the water. They played tag ball, had races, and finally the older children decided to dive from a large tree limb that hung out over the water. Harry went first, then Bert, Dorothy next, and finally it was Nan's turn.

"Here I go," she called, bouncing up and down on the limb.

But before she had a chance to dive, there was a cracking sound and the limb started to break off. Nan lost her balance and tumbled into the water. The limb fell down after her.

"Oh!" cried Mrs. Bobbsey, swimming quickly toward the spot.

To everyone's horror Nan did not rise to the surface. Her parents, as well as Harry and Bert, dived to look for her.

Harry saw his cousin first. She was caught among the limb's branches and trying desperately to free herself before her breath gave out. He reached forward, grabbed Nan's hand and yanked her away. Together they came to the surface.

Both gasped for breath and the others helped them to shore. It took Nan longer to revive, due to the shock, but in a few minutes she was all right.

"Thanks, Harry," she said. "I certainly was afraid I wasn't going to make it."

Dinah, who had been watching the scene with bated breath, heaved a sigh of relief. Then she went to the galley and prepared some

Nan lost her balance and tumbled into the water

hot broth for Nan. The captain swam over with it in a thermos bottle.

"Good old Dinah!" said Nan and waved her thanks to the kindly cook.

In a little while everyone swam back to the *Bluebird* and dressed for supper. Afterward the children gathered in the stern of the boat and at eight o'clock Captain McGinty joined them.

"Please tell us a story," Flossie begged.

"All right," he said. "I'll tell you one that happened many years ago when I was living in Maryland in a village located near Chesapeake Bay. Wonderful fishing and crabbing in that area," Captain McGinty said dreamily.

"Yes, yes!" Freddie prompted eagerly. "What did you do?"

"One day I went out fishing in a small rowboat. The fish weren't biting too well, so I rowed farther out until I reached the deep channel."

"What did you catch?" asked Freddie, climbing up on the captain's lap.

"More than I looked for!" the officer answered. "There was a tug on my line and I reeled it in. Suddenly I heard a horrible noise whirling around me. I looked up to see and—"

"You saw a whale!" interrupted Flossie excitedly. "Didn't you?"

"No. Guess again."

"A flock of birds?" Freddie suggested.

"No!" the captain said, then paused, flinging his arms out as if he were trying to ward off something. "It was a waterspout!"

"You mean someone had a hose and sprinkler in the water?" asked Flossie.

Captain McGinty smiled and explained to the children that a waterspout is the name given to a tornado when it occurs at sea. A waterspout is like a funnel-shaped cloud and the point of the funnel dips into the water. The water whirls around, sucking up the other water with it. Sometimes a waterspout is three hundred feet high.

"Did the water suck you up, too?" cried Nan.

"If it had I'd never be here to tell the story!" the officer laughed. Then he said seriously, "When I saw that old spout of water, I started to row. I rowed so hard I nearly wore out the two oars. Believe me, it was rough, for the current kept pulling me nearer to the spout."

"Go on . . ." urged Harry, as the captain paused for breath.

"I finally made it to shore. A lot of my friends were standing on the beach watching this strange spectacle. They pulled me out of the boat, because I was so weak and scared I couldn't move."

"I hope the waterspout didn't chase you up on the beach!" Flossie exclaimed.

"No." Captain McGinty took Freddie off his lap and stood up. "It ended soon after that—the big column of water just sort of exploded like a firecracker."

"I hope I never have an experience like that!" Harry exclaimed.

"I do, too!" Captain McGinty said. "But now, off to bed, you young folks. It's two bells," he said, hearing the nautical clock in his quarters strike. "To you, that's nine o'clock."

The children all went to bed and within a short while everyone aboard the *Bluebird* was sound asleep. Around midnight, Bert was awakened by a rocking sensation and a loud clap of thunder.

He threw his covers aside and hopped out of bed. Harry and Freddie had awakened also and joined Bert at the window. Rain was coming down in sheets and pouring in. Lightning slashed through the sky.

"Oh!" shouted Freddie as his brother closed the window.

As the *Bluebird* tossed about like a cork, there was a loud pounding on the door and the captain's voice suddenly rang out in the corridor:

"Put on your life belts! Everybody put on life belts!"

CHAPTER VIII

"ABANDON SHIP!"

"OH!" cried Freddie. "Is the boat going to sink?"

Bert could not answer this, but he was worried. Under the boys' bunks were extra life belts. He pulled them out and quickly helped Freddie into one of them. Then Bert and Harry put theirs on and they all went into the corridor.

The boat was rolling so hard, the boys kept banging first into one wall, then the other. It was impossible to walk straight.

Lights were on, and in a few moments Mr. and Mrs. Bobbsey and the girls appeared in the corridor. The captain, who seemed the most sure-footed of anyone, made his way from the galley, which he had gone to inspect.

"Everybody all right?" he asked.

"Y-yes," all the children said, and Mr. Bobbsey asked, "Do you think there's any danger, Captain?"

The officer said he did not want to frighten

anyone, but the thunderstorm was a bad one.

"If it strikes us," he said, "we may have to take to the lifeboats."

Suddenly Nan realized that Dinah and Snap and Snoop were not with them. Staggering precariously down the corridor, Nan managed to make her way to Dinah's cabin and pounded loudly on the door.

"Are you all right, Dinah?" she asked.

There was a groan from inside. Nan did not wait for an invitation to come in. She opened the door and snapped on the light. Dinah lay in her bed, rolling from side to side. Snoop and Snap were with her.

"Oh my!" the cook said in a tremulous voice. "I knew I never should've come on this trip. Old Dinah's just a landlubber. I feel awful sick."

Nan had to smile in spite of herself. She reached under Dinah's bunk and brought out a life belt which she helped the cook to adjust. By this time Mrs. Bobbsey had come to the doorway and advised that perhaps Dinah should stay in bed.

"In fact, maybe all of us would be more comfortable lying down," she said. "We'll keep the life belts on, though."

For the next half hour everyone except Mr. Bobbsey and the captain lay wide awake, wondering and worrying. The storm continued its fury, with the rain slashing at the windows and the rolling houseboat creaking and groaning in every seam.

All this time Captain McGinty and Mr. Bobbsey kept going from place to place to check the *Bluebird*. Finally the storm subsided. The thunder and lightning stopped, the rain became a pleasant pitter-patter, and the houseboat ceased to toss about. She had weathered the tempest!

"Pretty seaworthy old boat," said Bert to Harry from his bunk.

"She sure is," his cousin replied.

At last everyone went to sleep, but the next morning they could talk of nothing but the storm. The children declared it was the worst one they could remember.

"For a while I thought there was going to be a hurricane," said Captain McGinty. "We're lucky it wasn't."

Freddie asked him what the worst storm was he had ever been in, and the officer said it was a typhoon. One time when he was on a boat trip, a wall of water, caused by the terrific wind, had nearly capsized the ship.

"I never want to get into a typhoon again," the captain said, then changed the subject. "There is a big clean-up job to do this morning. Seamen Flossie and Freddie will swab the decks thoroughly."

The little twins looked at the captain in dismay. They had already been outside and seen the litter on deck. After the rain had stopped the night before, the wind had continued to blow. It had come from the land side and had left bits of twigs, leaves, and mud on the *Bluebird*. But the small twins would not for the world complain.

"Come on, Freddie," Flossie urged.

The children went for brooms and mops. They got to work with a will and Freddie whispered to his twin, "Maybe if we do a good job, we'll be promoted."

Flossie nodded and pushed the mop back and forth. In about ten minutes they saw Nan and Dorothy coming toward them. With a smile, the two older girls picked up a broom and a mop and started to help. Within an hour the deck was spic and span once more.

When Captain McGinty came around on his usual morning inspection, the twins waited eagerly to hear if they had won the promotion. But he merely told them they had done a good job and then called loudly:

"Time for boat drill! Everybody forward in bathing suits!"

The children scampered off to change their clothes. When all the passengers were assembled, the captain told them that there would be a demonstration of unpacking the self-inflating lifeboats and getting them into the water.

He ordered Bert and Harry to take the rubber boats from a locker. The boys laid the small, compact packages on the deck and unfolded them. They noticed a cylindrical cartridge which was attached at one end to the gunwales. Captain McGinty explained that it contained a gas.

"Now turn those valves on them," he ordered. "That'll fill 'em up so they'll float."

In a moment the circular gunwales swelled up. Now the rubber objects looked like boats and were ready for launching.

Freddie and Flossie, who had never seen such a boat, looked on in amazement. "I wish I had stuff like that to blow up my balloons and bicycle tires," said Freddie.

The boats were lowered over the side of the deck and the captain steadied first one, then the other, with a long pole.

"Who wants to jump first?" he asked.

There was a chorus of "I do!" from all the children. Captain McGinty decided it was best for the older ones to go first.

"Suppose we have a boys' boat and a girls' boat," he suggested.

Harry jumped first, teetered a bit, then sat down. Bert went next, and finally Freddie.

"There's a paddle under the gunwale," the officer told them.

Bert pulled out the paddle, which was collapsible. He quickly unfolded it and steadied the rubber boat with it. Then he pushed off a little distance from the other boat.

One by one, the three girls jumped down into their boat. Flossie, who was the last, almost did not make it. She landed on the side and nearly fell into the water. But Nan caught her and pulled the little girl inside. Dorothy picked up the little paddle, and the two boats were

paddled around in the water for several minutes.

"Let's have a race to the shore and back,"
Dorothy proposed.

"Okay," said Bert. "Go!"

Dorothy and Harry paddled while the others
used their hands to push the water and help the
rubber boats glide along. The girls reached the
shore first, but on the way back the boys over-
took them and won the race.

"All aboard!" Captain McGinty shouted
presently.

The boys, being nearer the *Bluebird,* pulled
up first. Freddie climbed the ladder, then the
two older boys. Dorothy now steered her rubber boat close. Flossie went up and climbed
over the rail followed by her sister.

Dorothy noticed that Captain McGinty was
not watching her—in fact, he was not even in
sight. A mischievous look came into her eyes.
She would paddle around just a bit longer.

When she was about twenty feet from the
houseboat, the captain suddenly appeared at
the rail. He was about to scold Dorothy, when
suddenly everyone heard a loud hissing sound.
The gas was leaking out of the rubber boat!

"Abandon ship!" the officer commanded
Dorothy.

"Glug!" said Dorothy, as girl and boat disappeared under the surface of the lake.

CHAPTER IX

TWO YOUNG HEROES

EVERYBODY on board the *Bluebird* laughed loudly as Dorothy Minturn disappeared under the water, still seated in the lifeboat. Everybody, that is, except Captain McGinty. His brow furrowed and his eyes narrowed.

Nan, catching sight of him, stopped giggling and began to worry. She knew some type of punishment was going to be meted out to her cousin!

Dorothy knew this, too. The instant she had made her saucy remark, she had caught sight of the captain's stern face. But it was too late to change her mind. As she went under water, Dorothy began to figure out how she could avoid punishment.

"I know what I'll do," she told herself. "I'll save the lifeboat!"

This was easier said than done. Though Dorothy was a strong girl, she did not find it easy to bring the boat to the surface. She lost her hold on it and had to come to the surface for air.

As her head appeared, those on deck expected Dorothy to swim to the *Bluebird* and come aboard. But instead, she disappeared under the water once more. By this time the rubber boat was gone down several more feet. It was near the bottom of the lake.

"Oh dear!" Dorothy thought. "I never can get it!"

Needing air, she swam to the surface again and took a deep breath. Near her the paddle was floating toward shore. Dorothy went after it. Then bringing it near the houseboat, she gave the paddle a high toss. Harry caught it.

"We must rescue the lifeboat," she called. "Harry and Bert, will you come and help me? I can't bring it to the surface alone."

Captain McGinty had been about to speak but suddenly changed his mind. He disappeared inside the cabin.

The boys were overboard in a minute. Dorothy directed them to the sunken lifeboat and soon the three had brought it to the surface. Then, between the three of them, they managed to haul it up the ladder to the deck of the *Bluebird*.

Everyone was loud in his praise of Dorothy. She did not smile, however. She was unhappy for several minutes, fully expecting Captain McGinty to come and scold her. When he did not appear she finally relaxed.

Mr. Bobbsey and the captain decided that they would move the *Bluebird* directly after lunch. They would go to Lemby Creek and anchor.

"That's the place where Bruce Watson lives, isn't it, Daddy?" Nan asked. "Maybe we'll see him."

Nan asked her father what he thought might be done about helping the boy, who had indicated he was mistreated by his stepfather. Mr. Bobbsey said the case would have to be thoroughly investigated before anything could be done.

"But," he added, "if Bruce is not getting enough to eat and is being overworked, I shall certainly do something about that."

"Oh, that's wonderful!" said Nan. "Do you suppose we could find out about Bruce while we're at Lemby Creek?" Her father was not sure this would be possible, but promised to do what he could.

Mr. Bobbsey now went to inspect the engine to be sure everything was in order after the storm. Captain McGinty had gone to his quarters to write up the ship's log. Mrs. Bobbsey and the older children busied themselves at various tasks. Only Flossie and Freddie found themselves with nothing to do.

"Let's play with Snoop and Snap," the little girl suggested.

But the cat, who was sunning himself on the deck, did not want to play. Neither did Snap. He had had a big breakfast and was more in the mood for a morning nap than a romp.

"I know what," said Freddie. "Let's play fire. I'll fill my pumper with water and we'll take it down in the hold and pretend there's a fire."

Usually Flossie did not care to play fire-fighting games with her twin. But suddenly she had an idea that maybe by using the pumper they could sprinkle water on the floor of the hold and then mop it up.

"That'll make it nice and clean," she said. "Then maybe we'll get our promotion."

Freddie agreed. He went to his cabin and dragged out the pumper. At a tap in the galley he filled it with water. Then he and Flossie dragged the pumper to the stairway and down into the hold.

The two children were wearing their sailor caps but hoped soon to have these exchanged for the officers' type. Or if this were not possible, at least they might have some kind of insignia put on their sweaters.

Reaching the foot of the stairway, Freddie suddenly sniffed. Could it possibly be that he smelled smoke? The little boy looked all around but could see no sign of any flames.

A moment later Flossie said, "I smell smoke, but I don't see any fire."

"Maybe it's upstairs," said Freddie excitedly and dashed back up the steps.

He was right! Something in the galley was burning! He knew Dinah was not there. She was cleaning the main cabin.

Flossie was at her twin's heels, and the two children dashed into the galley. There was a fire indeed! Someone had left the hot plate plugged in, and a newspaper lying near it had ignited and was now in flames.

Freddie, the little fireman, knew exactly what to do. He grabbed a large pan, filled it with water, and threw it on the flames.

"It's going out!" Freddie cried gleefully. "But we'll have to work faster! Wish I had time to get my pumper."

In his excitement the little boy climbed into the sink and hurled water onto the fire by the handful. Still there were flames, and suddenly the little boy realized that the woodwork along the side of the counter had caught fire.

His twin grabbed up a box of salt and tore off the top. As Freddie continued to splash water onto the fire, Flossie threw the salt onto it. Finally the flames vanished.

"It's out! It's out!" Freddie cried triumphantly.

At this moment the twins heard running footsteps in the corridor, and a moment later Dinah appeared.

"Oh, lawsy me!" she exclaimed. "What you-all doing?"

Flossie explained, and poor Dinah looked woebegone. "It's all my fault! It's all my fault!" she wailed.

The cook confessed that she had left the hot plate on. Someone had brought in the newspaper and laid it too close to the heat, without knowing that the electricity was on.

The commotion now brought everyone including the captain to the galley. Dinah shamefacedly told her story again, and Mr. Bobbsey admitted that he had been the one to lay the newspaper near the hot plate.

Mrs. Bobbsey hugged the small twins. "You are real heroes!" she said.

Captain McGinty stepped forward. "Indeed they are," he said. "Freddie and Flossie, I believe you have earned promotions. Freddie, I hereby appoint you Chief Fireman. Flossie, your rating will be Fireman First Class."

"Oh, thank you!" the twins cried together. Flossie added, "Will we change our caps now?"

Mrs. Bobbsey spoke up, smiling. "I wish you would keep those little sailor caps," she said. "I'm sure they are more becoming than officers' caps."

Freddie said he did not care what kind of a cap he wore, but he would like an insignia. Nan laughed and said that she had bought two extra ones, hoping that Freddie would be appointed Chief Fireman.

She ran off to get them, and presented Freddie with his. She also handed one to Flossie, and while it had nothing to do with fire-fighting, Flossie said this did not matter.

"Why, it's for a nurse," she remarked, and her older sister nodded.

Captain McGinty smiled broadly. "Then I'll change your rating, Flossie," he said. "You will be Chief Nurse."

Dinah now asked that everyone leave the galley so that she might clean up the mess the fire had made. Nan and Dorothy, however, remained to help her. In a short time everything was clean and lunch was started.

At twelve o'clock Nan and Dorothy went on deck to summon everyone to come and eat. To their amazement, the sky had become overcast.

"Oh dear," said Dorothy, "is it going to rain again?"

"Well, if it does, I hope it won't be anything like last night," said Nan.

At this moment Harry came dashing from his cabin out onto the deck. There was a look of fright in the boy's eyes. He explained that he had been listening in on his short-wave radio set and had just heard a weather report.

"It was a storm warning," he said excitedly. "A typhoon is headed this way!"

CHAPTER X

A CRUEL MAN

AT HARRY'S announcement of a typhoon, the *Bluebird* became a scene of confusion. The children ran back and forth, peering into the sky and across the water with frightened eyes. Snap barked excitedly.

"We'd better go ashore fast!" Bert exclaimed. "The boat'll be swamped!"

"Let's hurry!" said Flossie, running to her mother's side. "I'm 'fraid of tie-funs!"

Captain McGinty's commanding drawl broke through the noise. "Hold on there, Harry! Where did this weather report come from?"

A blank look appeared on Harry's face, as he felt everyone's attention focused on him.

"I—I forgot to find out, but I'll go back and ch-check," he stammered.

Harry dashed off to the Communications Shack and tuned in his short-wave set again. While he was gone, Flossie picked up her dolls, Nan found Snoop, and Freddie stood by the rail.

"I'm ready to 'bandon ship," he said.

In a few moments Harry returned to the cabin. The youth walked up to the group slowly with a sheepish expression on his face.

"Well?" inquired the captain, as his Communications Officer approached him.

"I'm afraid I made a mistake!" Harry admitted in an unusually quiet voice. "The report was from Honolulu!"

"Hawaii?" squeaked Freddie, looking at his cousin in surprise.

"Yes!" Harry said, his face a bright crimson shade. He looked out over the water with his arms folded in back of him.

"Well, blow me down!" Captain McGinty said heartily. "The Communications Officer had better study some navigation with us, eh, Mr. Bobbsey?"

"Harry sure pulled a Lulu! A Hono-Lulu!" Bert exclaimed, taunting his good-natured cousin.

Harry covered his ears, trying to avoid hearing the laughter that followed, and the captain explained that typhoons never occur on lakes in the eastern United States. He added that he thought they would have to postpone sailing until the next morning.

"The Chief Cook has reported that we need more supplies," he said.

Mrs. Bobbsey looked surprised, then she suddenly realized why. Captain McGinty had an enormous appetite! Dinah had reported that the refrigerator had been raided several times.

"I'll go to town," Mr. Bobbsey offered. "Millville isn't far inland."

"Please, may I go too?" Freddie asked. "I have to buy something."

"What?" Flossie wanted to know.

He drew his twin aside and whispered in her ear. She giggled. To the others he said, "It's a secret."

His father consented, and they set off in the little dinghy which the houseboat carried. Hours later they returned with various packages of food. The others waited to see Freddie's surprise but he said nothing about it.

Bert and Harry were fishing. Dinah had said teasingly that it was strange nobody had caught anything yet—they had not had one fish dinner on board to date! The boys were determined to catch a trout or a bass.

Freddie brought out his line but went to the other side of the deck. Flossie joined him. A few minutes later he gave a yell. When the boys rushed to his side, he proudly said, "See!"

In a glass bowl alongside Freddie swam a large goldfish.

"You—you caught that?" Bert asked.

Freddie just grinned. "Have you caught anything yet?"

The boys admitted they had not. Then Harry winked at Bert. "I guess we'll have to eat your goldfish for supper, Freddie."

"Oh, no!" shrieked Flossie. "Goldfish aren't meant to eat. They're just to look pretty. Freddie said the man in the store—"

Flossie had not meant to give away her twin's secret. "So you bought it, eh?" quizzed Harry.

When Freddie admitted he had, Bert laughed heartily.

"You had me fooled for a moment. It was a good joke," he chuckled.

Just before bedtime the family usually gathered in the main cabin. Now all were there but Nan and Dorothy.

"Where are they?" Mrs. Bobbsey asked.

"I'll look in our room," Flossie offered.

"Get ready for bed while you're there," her mother said.

Flossie skipped down the corridor and went into her cabin. Neither Nan nor Dorothy was there. "That's funny," the little girl thought. "Where could they be?"

Quickly the little girl put on her pajamas and striped bathrobe. Just as she was about to cross to the door, she heard it being opened.

"I'll fool them," thought Flossie and darted into the closet, leaving the door open a wee crack.

Nan and Dorothy walked into the room,

whispering. Flossie could see that they were holding a white bundle. "You're so clever, Dorothy!" Nan exclaimed.

Dorothy chuckled. "Serves 'em right for beating us in the rubber boat race."

Flossie opened the closet door a little farther, for she was suffocating from heat. Suddenly she lost her balance and clutched for the doorknob. But she missed it and tumbled out onto the floor.

"Oh!" Nan exclaimed, whirling around.

Flossie quickly got up. "I really scared you!" she giggled. "But what's in that bundle, Nan?"

"You'll find out later, Flossie," her sister replied, "but let's go to bed now. I'm tired!"

They ran off to say good night to the others but were soon back. As the girls climbed into their bunks, they heard Freddie, Bert, and Harry going into the Communications Shack. A short while later, yells and shouts came from the boys' cabin.

Nan and Dorothy hopped out of their bunks and opened the door to the corridor. Flossie sat up and watched curiously as the older girls tried to suppress giggles.

Mr. and Mrs. Bobbsey, meanwhile, had rushed to the Communications Shack and burst in.

"We've been short-sheeted, and there are frogs in our bunks!" Bert cried.

"And we know who did it!" Harry added. "There are the culprits!" He pointed at the doorway.

Nan and Dorothy were peering in, looking very innocent. "Why, what do you mean?" Dorothy asked.

"You took off our bottom sheets and fixed the top ones to look like two," said Freddie. "We couldn't get in any farther than our knees!"

"And you added the frogs," accused Harry and he slipped one down Dorothy's back. "You can have him for a pet!"

The boys roared as Dorothy wriggled and squealed.

Finally the frogs were dropped overboard, the boys' beds were made properly, and everyone settled down for a peaceful night.

Next day, Freddie was up early to raise the flag. He was very proud of this duty and had not missed performing it once. The other children joined the little boy on deck shortly afterward and looked at the morning sun.

"It's going to be a scorcher today!" Harry exclaimed. "Especially for some people."

The others knew he meant Nan and Dorothy. The boys were sure to try to get square for the prank the girls had played on them.

The girls pretended not to understand. "Yes, I guess it will be warm today," Nan said. "Good for a suntan."

"You'll get tanned all right!" Bert threatened, a double meaning in his words.

"Breakfast!" called Dinah, banging on the dishpan.

The children ate a hearty meal of grapefruit, hot cereal, blueberry muffins, and large glasses of milk. Captain McGinty added to this, eggs, sausage, and coffee, and he had two helpings of each. Afterward, he went up to the wheelhouse and the *Bluebird* started its journey toward Lemby Creek. They would go through this to Lake Arrow.

During the next few hours, Bert and Harry kept to themselves. Nan and Dorothy were worried about what the boys would do in return for the trick they had played on them.

Around four o'clock that afternoon, the *Bluebird* reached Lemby Creek. Captain McGinty had been letting the children take turns steering the boat, but now he took over. There was a slight current at the spot where Lake Metoka joined Lemby Creek, and the captain did not want the *Bluebird* to go aground.

In a little while the houseboat had been safely turned into the narrow creek. At times the shores were so close that overhanging tree branches brushed the rails of the *Bluebird*. But presently the houseboat moved out from the wooded part of the creek to a place where wide meadows stretched on either side.

Going around a bend in the stream, the Bobbseys came in sight of a farmhouse, barn, and several other buildings located near it.

"What a pretty farm!" Nan exclaimed.

"Yes, and it belongs to Mr. Hardman, I think," said Mr. Bobbsey. "We can tie up our boat at his dock and see if he'll sell us some fresh eggs and milk."

"And we can ask Bruce how he's getting along," Nan said.

"Look! There's Bruce now!" Freddie shouted in delight. "He's fishing."

The farm boy was so intent on his fishing, he had not yet noticed the houseboat coming.

"We may as well tie up here for the night," Mr. Bobbsey said as they reached a place where four stakes had been driven into the ground. "That will give us a chance to talk to Bruce. And," he added, winking at Bert and Harry, "maybe Bruce can give you fellows some pointers on catching fish."

Bruce now glanced their way and saw the *Bluebird*. He waved excitedly at the children and stood up. The boy laid down his fishing pole and had just started for the boat, when Nan cried out:

"Look!"

A mean-looking man dressed in overalls had come up behind Bruce with a strap in his hands. He grabbed the boy by one shoulder.

"This'll teach you to loaf on the job!" he shouted, bringing the strap down across Bruce's back.

"Stop him!" Nan pleaded frantically. "Oh, please stop him, Daddy!"

CHAPTER XI

A MYSTERIOUS NOISE

MR. BOBBSEY made a flying leap over the railing of the boat and landed on the shore. Quickly he ran through the tall grass along the waterfront as Bruce cried out piteously.

The farmer who was beating Bruce did not see Mr. Bobbsey coming. He jumped when the twins' father cried out angrily:

"Drop that strap!"

The farmer whirled around, his fist tightening on the strap. "Mind your own business!" he snarled.

"Why, Mr. Hardman!" Mr. Bobbsey said in astonishment, recognizing the man. He had once sold some lumber to him. "I can hardly believe you would do such a thing!"

Mr. Hardman did not acknowledge that he knew Mr. Bobbsey by so much as a flicker in his beady eyes. Instead, he turned toward Bruce and lifted the strap again, as if to strike the sobbing boy.

"Give me that strap!" shouted Mr. Bobbsey,

and snatched it from the other man's hand.

"Why, you—I'll teach you not to meddle in my business!" Mr. Hardman screeched. He clenched his fists and charged toward Mr. Bobbsey.

From the deck of the *Bluebird* the six children, Mrs. Bobbsey, and the captain were watching anxiously.

"Oh! That man is going to hurt Daddy!" sobbed Flossie, clutching Nan's hand.

"No, he isn't, Flossie!" Bert exclaimed, picking up his little sister so she could see better. "Dad can take care of himself!"

"Just look at Uncle Richard!" yelled Harry with delight.

Mr. Bobbsey had stood his ground calmly. When Mr. Hardman reached him, he ducked, then used a judo trick he had learned years before at college. The surprised farmer tumbled right over Mr. Bobbsey's shoulders and landed in the water.

"Hurrah for you, Dad!" cheered Bert, and the children clapped their hands joyously.

The farmer got to his feet and splashed out of the water, his face purple with rage.

"When you cool off," Mr. Bobbsey said to him, "we'll discuss this situation." He turned to Bruce, who was watching his stepfather fearfully. "Let me see those welts." There was concern in his voice. "Hm-m, some of these cuts are pretty deep. You had better come aboard the *Bluebird* and let Mrs. Bobbsey rub some ointment on your back."

"Thank you, sir, but I can take care of them," Bruce replied gratefully. "If I come aboard, he'll be madder than ever."

"I'm going to help you, Bruce," Mr. Bobbsey promised. He looked up to see Mr. Hardman climbing up the bank of the creek. The cruel man was dripping wet and his eyes snapped.

"Think you're a tin hero, don't you?" the farmer addressed Mr. Bobbsey. "And you, you little cheat," he added, glaring at Bruce, "get up to the barn!"

"Exactly what did the boy do?" asked Mr. Bobbsey in a stern voice.

"Fishing—loafing—when he should be working!" Mr. Hardman murmured in a furious tone.

"I only fished before I was going to do the milking," Bruce said defensively. He looked at Mr. Bobbsey quickly. "I'd better do what my stepfather says." With that, the unhappy boy turned and ran toward a large barn.

"And you, Bobbsey, stay out of my affairs," added Mr. Hardman, admitting that he had recognized Mr. Bobbsey. "Furthermore, get your boat and your family off my property immediately, or you'll be sorry!"

"This is a public waterway," the twins' father said calmly. Anyhow, I'm going to report your treatment of Bruce to the proper authorities. You haven't heard the end of this, Mr. Hardman. Good day!" Mr. Bobbsey stalked off and returned to the *Bluebird*.

"Did he hurt Bruce very much?" Flossie asked anxiously, as her father climbed on deck. Tears were streaming down the little girl's chubby cheeks and Nan's eyes, too, were damp.

"No, he's going to be all right!" Mr. Bobbsey said reassuringly.

"Daddy, you're not a tin hero," said Freddie. "You're a real one."

Captain McGinty spoke up in a deep voice. "I call that beating disgraceful. Who was that man, Mr. Bobbsey?"

"The lad's stepfather, a man named Hardman!"

"Oh!" said Bert, remembering what Bruce had started to tell them about his beatings when they first met.

"What can we do for Bruce?" Nan asked in concern.

"First thing tomorrow, I'll go into Lemby and check the town records," her father replied. "I'm curious to see if Bruce was ever legally adopted by Mr. Hardman. If he wasn't, then he becomes a ward of the state, under state protection. But, in either case, I am going to see the sheriff and report this incident," Mr. Bobbsey concluded thoughtfully.

Meanwhile Bert, Harry, and Dorothy had been talking about the clever judo trick Mr. Bobbsey had used.

"Uncle Richard sure fixed Mr. Hardman," Dorothy said with a laugh. "I'm going to ask him to teach that trick to me."

"Girls can't learn judo!" Harry exclaimed scornfully.

"Dorothy can do anything athletic!" Nan spoke up, throwing an affectionate arm around her cousin's waist.

"Ho-ho! We'll soon see just how *strong* you girls are!" said Bert with a grin, winking at Harry.

"How?" Dorothy asked.

"You'll find out later."

Supper was ready early and the family sat down with the captain to eat. But poor Flossie could only gaze at the appetizing food. The incident concerning Bruce had upset her so much that she had no interest in eating.

"I'll fix you up, honey child," Dinah said, hustling back to the galley.

From a shelf she took a bag in which was a special plate. Turning this over, Dinah wound a little key on the bottom of it. Then she filled the plate with food and carried it back to the table in the dining room.

"Here you are, Flossie," she said, taking away the little girl's regular plate and setting the new one down in front of her. "You just press hard on that food and see what happens!"

Flossie stuck her fork into a piece of chicken. Suddenly music began to come from the plate!

"You'll have to eat steady like to hear the whole tune," said Dinah.

Everyone else stopped eating to watch Flossie, whose face had lighted up as if by magic. In a few minutes meat, potato, and peas were gone to the tune of "Yankee Doodle"!

"Why, Dinah, that's awfully cute," said Nan. "Where did the plate come from?"

The cook chuckled. "I brought it along just in case any little folks lost their appetites." Then she went back to the galley.

Nan followed her and explained what had happened to Bruce, and kind-hearted Dinah said instantly, "That poor boy! He sure needs some o' Dinah's cookin' to fatten him up! I'm goin' to fix a plate of fried chicken right now an' take it up to him!"

Mrs. Bobbsey, who had come into the galley, thanked Dinah but explained that they had better not do anything until morning, after Mr. Bobbsey saw the sheriff.

For a while the family sat out on the deck of the houseboat, enjoying the beautiful June evening. From the Hardman farm they heard the occasional whinny of a horse, and once a dog barked for a few minutes. But there was nothing else to break the silence of the night except the melodious sound of Dinah's singing.

Flossie announced that she was going to bed early and Mrs. Bobbsey tucked her in her bunk and kissed her. The small girl had been unusually quiet and her mother thought it must be because of Bruce's misfortune.

Soon afterward, the other children said good night and in a short time were sound asleep. But in the middle of the night Bert was awakened by a mosquito buzzing around his head. He sat up in his bunk and tried to swat the small insect. But it escaped into the air. Bert slid down between the sheets again and started to doze off.

Bzzzzzz! The mosquito lighted on his arm.

"Ouch!" Bert said, sitting up with a start.

He hopped out of his bunk and fumbled for his flashlight. This time Bert got the mosquito, but now, wide awake, he felt hungry.

"Might as well get a glass of milk," he decided, and headed quietly for the galley.

The boy had almost reached it when he heard a bang not far away. Was someone else up? Bert listened, flashing his light around, but there were no footsteps. What had caused the mysterious sound?

Bert went into the galley and opened the refrigerator door. He took out a carton of milk. As he started to pour some into a glass, he heard another noise. This time it was muffled.

"Where is that coming from?" Bert asked himself.

Leaving the half-filled milk glass on the counter, Bert walked through the deserted corridor, the main cabin, and finally onto the deck. No one was up. He could hear snoring from the captain's quarters.

"Maybe some animal got on board," Bert decided.

He returned to the galley, filled the glass with milk, and raised it to his lips. Suddenly a frightened scream rang through the still air. He set down the glass and dashed back through the corridor.

"That sounded like Flossie!" he thought.

Mr. and Mrs. Bobbsey had heard the cry and dashed out of their own cabin and into that of the girls, just as Bert reached it.

The light was on now, and Nan and Dorothy were trying to comfort Flossie. She was sitting up in bed clutching the sheets, a look of terror on her face.

"I had a nightmare!" she was sobbing. "I dreamed that Mr. Hardman beat poor Bruce so badly that he had to go to the hospital. Oh, it was awful!"

"You're all right now, dear," said Mrs. Bobbsey in a soothing voice.

"Can I come in and sleep with you, Mommy?" the little girl asked. "I'm 'fraid."

"Certainly," her mother said, and Mr. Bobbsey carried Flossie into their cabin. Soon it was quiet again aboard the boat, except for the gentle slapping of waves against the sides of the houseboat.

The following morning Mr. Bobbsey said they would continue up the creek a short distance to the town of Lemby. He would then go to see the sheriff.

"Off we go," he called to the captain. "I'll start the engine." Then he noticed a strange look on Bert's face. "What's the matter, son?" he asked.

"Look there!" Bert pointed.

Just ahead, stretched across a narrow part of Lemby Creek was a strong wire fence, fastened to posts driven into the bottom of the stream.

The boat could go no farther on her voyage. The Bluebird's *course was barricaded!*

CHAPTER XII

THE RUNAWAY

CAPTAIN McGINTY and the Bobbseys stared in amazement at the wire fence blockade in the creek. Someone had put it up during the night to prevent their going any farther. But why?

"I'll bet Mr. Hardman did that!" said Bert. "He was plenty mad at us."

"I suspect he's the one," Mr. Bobbsey agreed. "Well, he'll take it down. I'm going ashore and find out!"

"Let me come, too," said Bert. "Mr. Hardman may be hiding near by."

"All right. And you too, Harry."

The three jumped to the shore and set off. They looked across the fields and in several of the farm buildings, but the owner was not in sight.

"He probably went to town," said Harry.

"And took Bruce with him," Bert added. "What'll we do, Dad?"

"If we don't find Mr. Hardman, we'll bor-

96

row some tools and cut the fence down. But that will mean getting to Lemby late and the sheriff probably will have left his office."

By this time the group was marching to the house. They had little hope of finding the farmer there at this hour. But to their amazement he was seated on a bench in the rear yard, staring into space.

As the three Bobbseys approached, he looked up. At once his faraway expression turned to a look of hate. He rose and started for the door but Mr. Bobbsey stopped him.

"Did you put up that fence in the creek, Mr. Hardman?" he asked.

"Yes! Put it up last night with the help of a couple of my friends. I warned you to leave my property yesterday."

"But we want to go on up the creek," Bert burst out. "You have no right to try to stop us. This is a public creek."

"Maybe it is, in certain places," said Mr Hardman, "but here the creek runs through my land. I own fields on both sides of it, so I own the creek in between. If I don't want to let you through, I don't have to!"

"But why won't you?" Mr. Bobbsey asked.

"Because you've interfered in my business. Furthermore, if you do anything to damage my fence I'll have you put in jail for destruction of property! Now back your boat out of here!"

"Just a moment, please, Mr. Hardman!" said a strange voice, and a tall, well-dressed man wearing a dark summer suit and straw hat came around the corner of the house.

"Why, hello, Mr. Weston!" Mr. Bobbsey exclaimed, recognizing him as the president of a bank in Lakeport. He introduced the newcomer to his son and nephew and Mr. Hardman.

Mr. Weston cleared his throat and said, "I know Mr. Hardman well. I'm sorry to eavesdrop, but I couldn't help overhearing the conversation. What seems to be the trouble, Mr. Hardman?"

The farmer looked down at the ground and said the Bobbseys had annoyed him and made trouble between him and his stepson. "They've got no right to come here. This is my home and I'll do as I please in it!"

"It won't be your home long if you don't pay back the money you borrowed from the bank," said Mr. Weston. "You haven't been near us for months."

The farmer seemed uneasy. "Well, to tell you the truth," he said, "I haven't got that money just now, Mr. Weston. Times have been hard, and crops are poor, and I'm sort of low on cash."

"I'm sorry, Mr. Hardman, but you didn't keep your promise. The reason you can't make

any money here is because you won't hire a man
or two to help you."

The Bobbseys looked at one another. Mr.
Hardman must be expecting ten-year-old Bruce
to do the work of two men!

"The Board of Directors of the bank," Mr.
Weston went on, "have decided to take owner-
ship of this farm until back payments and interest on the loan are paid up."

"Oh, don't do that!" Mr. Hardman begged.
"I'll raise the money. I'll get a hired man. I'll
pay off some of the loan in another six months."

"I'm sorry, Mr. Hardman, but we have given
you extra time before and you haven't kept your
bargain. This time—you must pay within one
month or leave here. You can live on the farm
until then," the banker concluded.

"Those are impossible terms!" Mr. Hardman shouted angrily, a flush creeping up
around his neck.

"And while I think of it, you had better take
down that fence immediately so Mr. Bobbsey's boat can continue on its journey!" Mr.
Weston said firmly.

Mr. Bobbsey thanked the bank president,
and Harry and Bert raised their arms in a
silent cheer.

Suddenly Mr. Hardman exclaimed, "All
right! All right. I'll be glad to get the entire
Bobbsey family and their boat out of my sight.

If it weren't for them, my stepson wouldn't have run away!"

"Bruce ran away?" Bert asked in astonishment. "When?"

Mr. Bobbsey and Harry also began to question Mr. Hardman about this, but the man stalked into the house and slammed the door. Mr. Weston asked the others to tell him why they were being blamed.

"It was because I interfered when Mr. Hardman was beating Bruce," Mr. Bobbsey explained.

"Well, I suppose the authorities will find the boy and bring him back," Mr. Weston said, and added, "I must be going now."

Mr. Bobbsey thanked him for his help, then he and the two boys went back to the *Bluebird*. There they told the captain and the others the results of the meeting.

"Bruce is gone!" they cried, on hearing the news.

Everyone tried to figure out where he could be. It was their opinion that the boy must have found out his uncle's address and gone to him.

"I'm glad," Nan murmured.

"Me, too," said Flossie. "Now I won't have any more bad dreams about Bruce."

In a short while they saw Mr. Hardman bring a man to the creek. Together they cut the fence, pulled up the stakes, and carted them away. They did not speak to anyone on board nor even look in their direction.

Captain McGinty went to the wheelhouse and soon the *Bluebird* was under way. At three o'clock the travelers reached the town of Lemby, at the end of the creek. The houseboat was docked and Mrs. Bobbsey and Dinah went ashore to do some marketing. Mr. Bobbsey decided that even though Bruce had run away, he would check the courthouse records regarding him just the same. It was possible the boy might be brought back to his cruel stepfather, and then the same trouble would be in store for Bruce.

"In that case, I'll report the situation," he told the children.

He went into town and at supper told the result of his investigation to the others. It appeared that Bruce had never been adopted by Mr. Hardman. Apparently the farmer had assumed guardianship of Bruce without going through the proper court procedure.

"Well, I hope he'll be happy now, wherever he is," said Nan.

After supper Harry said, "Bert, let's listen in on the short-wave set."

"Okay. We might even get a report on Bruce."

"Fine!" his cousin agreed, and the two boys retired to the Communications Shack.

"Oh!" screamed Nan. "There's a skeleton in my closet!"

The rest of the family went to the main cabin and persuaded Mrs. Bobbsey to play the piano for them while they sang seagoing songs. Their voices rang through the stillness in the quiet inlet.

"I'm going to get a coat," said Nan awhile later. "This air is chilly when the sun goes down."

The girls' cabin was dark as she entered, for someone had drawn the blinds. But the light from the corridor was sufficient for Nan to find her way to the closet. She opened the door, remembering that she had left her blue jacket hanging on a peg.

"Oh!" Nan screamed a second later, looking at the most terrifying sight she had ever seen.

She darted into the corridor, colliding with Bert and Harry. The slender girl was trembling with fear.

"There—there's—a skeleton in my—closet!" she shrieked.

CHAPTER XIII

A CALL FOR HELP

"A SKELETON in your closet?" Bert exclaimed. "Let's see it."

"You can look if you want to," his twin said. "It's horrible. Take it out!"

By this time Dorothy had come on the run. "What's the matter?" she asked.

"Look in the closet," Nan quavered.

Her cousin looked from one boy to another, but they remained silent. Dorothy thought she caught a gleam of fun in Harry's eyes so, unafraid, she went into her cabin, followed by the boys. Seeing the dangling, glowing skeleton, she gasped.

"Ugh!" Dorothy said, then suddenly laughed.

Going up to the skeleton, she shook its bony hand. Then she took it from the closet and began to dance around the cabin with it.

"This old fellow is only made of paper—it's nothing but a charcoal outline of a skeleton. Look, Nan!"

"Thank goodness!" her cousin said in relief,

poking the paper gingerly. "And it's covered with luminous paint so it will glow in the dark."

"Where did you get the paint, boys?" Dorothy asked, looking craftily at the two schemers.

Bert and Harry were eyeing the ceiling, but suddenly Freddie appeared and laughed loudly. He said eagerly, "We found the paint in the hold. It's some the men used on the searchlights."

"So you were in on the trick, too, you little monkey," said Nan. "Well, you gave me a good scare."

"We'll forgive you," Dorothy laughed. "And I guess this makes us even now!"

"No more short sheets?" Harry said, "Or frogs?"

"Not one," Dorothy agreed. "But you boys got the best of the bargain."

"How come?" Bert asked.

Dorothy answered with a chuckle in her voice, "You know *short* sheets make the bed seem *longer!*"

The boys groaned, then burst into laughter.

"I don't get it!" Flossie said, looking at her twin brother.

"It's a corny joke," said Bert. "Don't try a short sheet on your bed, Floss."

"Corny, eh?" said Dorothy. "Okay. Just for that, I'll play another joke on you as soon as I get a chance!"

Without thinking, Dorothy took the skeleton out into the corridor and hung it on a nail. In the draft it began to sway. A moment later Dinah came from the galley. Seeing the skeleton, she shrieked.

"Oh, Dinah, I'm sorry," Dorothy cried. "It's only made of paper."

"Paper or no paper, I don't like that bony ghost," the cook said, shivering. "Tear him up and throw him overboard!"

"Oh, no, we might need him," said Bert, but he did take down the skeleton, fold it up, and put it in a drawer of his cabin.

The next morning during breakfast Dinah confronted the group at the table. "There's more'n a paper ghost on this here ship. I'm missing some cookies, milk, and a loaf of bread!" she exclaimed, counting the items on her fingers.

The children grinned and looked at Captain McGinty, whose appetite seemed to grow larger each day. And they all knew that he had been the last one up the night before.

"Wasn't me!" the officer denied, rolling his eyes at each one in turn. "I had a snack but only fruit and a piece of pie. But you know— every boat has a hungry ghost!"

"Ghost!" sneered Dinah. "You can't play the same trick twice on old Dinah. There's no ghost on this ship."

"Of course there isn't, Dinah!" Mr. Bobbsey said calmly. "What probably happened was that a hungry thief crept aboard while we were sleeping and helped himself to the food."

Mrs. Bobbsey suggested that after this they keep the outside cabin door locked whenever they were in port, and her husband agreed.

When breakfast was over, Bert followed Captain McGinty on deck and helped him untie the ropes from the dock and pull up anchor. Soon the *Bluebird* sailed out of the small harbor and into the mouth of Lake Arrow.

"May I steer for a while?" Bert asked.

"Aye, mate," the officer answered.

Captain McGinty made up his cot while Bert handled the wheel. Then, after rummaging in his steamer trunk for a few minutes, the captain came into the wheelhouse with a bunch of small hand flags of various colors.

"Look, mate! Semaphore flags! I thought perhaps you older children might like to learn the ship-to-shore communication system. That is, if your dad will take the wheel for a while!"

Bert was delighted. "Nan and I first, Captain. Harry is teaching Dorothy how to act as his relief at the short-wave set right now. And I'll ask Dad to steer."

In a few minutes everything was set. Nan and Bert stood on deck ready for their lesson. Flossie and Freddie sat near by.

Captain McGinty explained that messages and signals were sent by hand flags. Each letter of the alphabet and the numbers one to ten called for a particular position of the arms.

"Say, this is terrific!" exclaimed Bert, going from A to Z several times. Then he spelled out *Bluebird* with the flags.

"Wish I could try it!" Freddie said wistfully.

"You can't spell well 'nuff, Freddie," his twin replied teasingly.

"I know something you can try," said Bert. "The signal that's a call for help—SOS."

He took his little brother aside and showed him how to semaphore the distress call.

"Look, Flossie!" Freddie said proudly, and showed his twin.

"I guess you can do anything, Freddie, if you try," she said, hugging him.

While Flossie and Freddie went to play, Bert, Nan, Harry, and Dorothy, who had joined them, practiced with the semaphore flags. They tried signaling to several boats, but none of them answered back.

"I wish we could talk to someone with the flags," said Bert.

The four children went into the cabin and sat down to play a guessing game. Suddenly Freddie came dashing in, crying excitedly:

"There's an SOS! Ship in trouble!"

"That's a good game to play," said Nan.

"It's not a game! I mean it! Come here!" Freddie urged.

The four older children followed him out on the port side. Some distance across the lake and about a quarter of a mile astern was another houseboat. A figure in white was using hand flags.

"You're right, Freddie," said Bert. "It *is* an SOS!"

He shouted up to the wheelhouse, directing Captain McGinty's attention to the distress signal. In a moment the *Bluebird* came to a shuddering halt.

"Find out what's the matter on that ship, mate," the captain ordered. "See if they really need help."

Bert ran for the flags and signaled, "We will come if you need us."

The other houseboat sent a message, "We are out of gas."

By this time Mr. Bobbsey had joined the children and was praising Freddie. The captain started up again, turned the *Bluebird,* and moved across Lake Arrow.

Bert signaled to the strange boat, "Who are you?"

A few seconds later Bert received a reply. He watched the signals carefully and reported:

"I think the boat is called the *Heron,* from Lemby. And I spelled the family's name as Clifton."

"I'll bet that's Jim Clifton's boat!" Mr. Bobbsey exclaimed. "Last time I talked to him, he told me that he had a houseboat, too. Signal back and tell them our name, son."

Fifteen minutes later the two houseboats met side by side in mid-lake. Captain McGinty cut the motor of the *Bluebird.*

"Dick Bobbsey!" shouted a short, roly-poly man dressed in white slacks and polo shirt. With him were a woman, a boy of sixteen, and a girl a little older.

"Hi, Jim!" grinned the twins' father. "Odd place to meet, isn't it?" Mr. Bobbsey introduced his wife, the captain, the twins, and their cousins to his old friend.

"I'm certainly happy to meet the Bobbsey family," Mr. Clifton exclaimed. "This is Mrs. Clifton, my daughter Peggy, and my son Ralph," he added. "It's certainly lucky for us you saw our distress signal."

Mr. Bobbsey said he would give him enough fuel to carry the *Heron* to a filling station.

"We'll rig up our plank between the boats and carry it over," the captain said.

Mr. Clifton invited the Bobbseys to come aboard the *Heron* and look around. Captain McGinty asked Bert to fasten the mooring lines joining the bows and sterns of the two houseboats. Then the officer cranked the gangplank into position so it would stretch between the boats, forming a passageway.

Ralph and Peggy led the twins and their cousins around the *Heron,* while Mr. and Mrs. Bobbsey talked with their parents.

When the children returned to the deck, they discovered that a joint supper party had been planned. Dinah was going to prepare sandwiches and cool drinks and Mrs. Clifton would supply potato salad and dessert.

"Whoopee!" shouted Freddie, delighted with the thought of a picnic.

While supper preparations were going on, he went back on the *Bluebird* to help carry some of the food and incidentally beg a sandwich ahead of time.

The good-natured cook gave the little boy a chicken sandwich to eat and a plate of them to carry. He started happily across the gangplank.

Unknown to Freddie or anyone else, the mooring lines between the two boats had loosened and they were drifting about ten feet apart. This meant that the gangplank, too, no longer reached.

Freddie stalked across the wide board, contentedly munching his sandwich. He reached the end—and stepped off into thin air!

CHAPTER XIV

TOMAHAWK ISLAND

FREDDIE and the plate of sandwiches hit the water with a loud splash. It brought Flossie, who had been watching him, to the railing in an instant.

"Oh!" she cried. "Come quick, everybody!"

Both families aboard the *Heron* rushed to her side. She pointed into the water, where Freddie was just coming to the surface holding an empty plate.

"All the sandwiches are gone!" Flossie exclaimed.

At first they did not know what she meant and were a little concerned about Freddie's unexpected bath. But when they heard the truth some laughed, others groaned.

"Our supper's at the bottom of Arrow Lake!" Bert said in mock dismay.

By this time Dinah had appeared on the deck of the *Bluebird*. Hearing what had happened, she said, "Oh my! Oh my! Now poor Dinah's got to make more sandwiches!"

She went off, as Freddie started climbing up the ladder of the Bobbsey boat to put on dry clothes. Captain McGinty retied the mooring lines and put the plank in place. Soon supper was ready and everyone enjoyed the delightful meal.

Before bidding the Cliftons good night, the Bobbseys made another picnic date for the following morning. The plan was to go to a deserted island in the middle of Arrow Lake, taking the Bobbseys' barbecue grill with them for a hamburger and frankfurter broil.

"Now watch your step, everybody," Mr. Bobbsey warned as his family started across the plank. "No more dips today."

Everyone got across without a mishap, then the two houseboats were separated. "Good night! Good night!" they called, and the children added, "See you in the sun!"

As Nan was undressing in her cabin, with Flossie already asleep, she said to Dorothy, "I wonder if anything will happen tonight."

But nothing did—at least not to awaken the passengers on the *Bluebird*. Next morning at breakfast Dinah declared that several corn muffins, some ham, two oranges, and a carton of milk had disappeared.

"I know who took it," said Freddie. "And he's not a twin."

"Well that leaves you, Harry, and the captain and me," Mr. Bobbsey laughed. "But I'm not guilty—ate too much at supper to be interested."

"I was stuffed," Harry declared, grinning.

All eyes turned on Captain McGinty. He was not smiling. In fact, his face took on a sour look. Without a word he got up and left the table.

"Oh dear," said Nan, "I guess we hurt his feelings."

"But he didn't deny eating the food," Bert pointed out. "Why didn't he own up?"

Mr. and Mrs. Bobbsey were puzzled. Was the captain sensitive about his appetite, or was he innocent? Finally Mr. Bobbsey said, "We may have had a visitor last night who climbed aboard. It never occurred to me to lock the main cabin except in port."

The matter was left this way, but still everyone wondered. At nine o'clock the two houseboats started their leisurely cruise. Since it was a wide lake and there was no danger of colliding with anything, Captain McGinty allowed Freddie and Flossie to steer the *Bluebird* for the first time. Then, after they had finished, Nan and Dorothy took turns.

"It's easy," said Dorothy.

Living at the shore, she spent a lot of time in boats and felt she knew a lot about them. On a panel at the front of the wheelhouse were several knobs. The girl wondered what they were and read the initials on them. They were plain to her except one with an F on it.

"I'll turn it on and right off again," Dorothy told herself.

She reached forward and twisted the knob. Instantly a foghorn on top of the wheelhouse began to blow loudly. Dorothy giggled, and Nan did, too, as her cousin turned the knob back.

But the horn continued to blow raucously!

"Oh, goodness!" Dorothy cried. "Now I've done it!"

Captain McGinty came rushing back to the wheelhouse. "What's going on here?" he thundered, storming toward the row of knobs.

He tried to turn off the foghorn, but it continued to give its loud, hoarse cry. The officer glared at the girls. "We'll have the whole shore patrol out here," he shouted. "They'll report me for inefficiency. They'll—they'll—" The captain was too upset to go on.

He turned off the boat's motor, ordered the girls to their quarters, and pulled out a chest of tools. Nan and Dorothy hurried down the steps, where they met Mr. and Mrs. Bobbsey and the other children.

"Did we spring a leak?" Bert asked.

"No," said Dorothy and told what she had done. The girl had to shout because of the loud noise from the foghorn.

Mr. Bobbsey and the boys laughed uproariously, but Flossie looked frightened and Mrs. Bobbsey said, "I suppose it's dangerous to experiment with unknown gadgets. You might have brought us into worse trouble, Dorothy. And," she added, looking up at the wheelhouse, "you'd better obey the captain's order. Here he comes."

Nan and her cousin scooted to their cabin. In the meantime the foghorn kept on blowing. Ten minutes went by before the captain was able to fix a short-circuited wire and stop the noise. Finally the *Bluebird* began its journey once more.

Soon after the bellowing had started, Bert had noticed Ralph using the semaphore flags. He realized the message was for the *Bluebird*.

"Are you in trouble?" it asked.

Bert went for his flags and replied, telling what had happened.

"Ha! Ha!" Ralph signaled back.

At noon the houseboats met at the island known as *Tomahawk Island*. The two families rowed ashore in their dinghys and pulled them up on a pebble-strewn beach.

Mr. Bobbsey and Mr. Clifton set up the barbecue grill while the boys unloaded the supplies. Mrs. Bobbsey and Mrs. Clifton helped Dinah unpack the picnic hampers. As Nan watched her father cooking frankfurters, she said:

"Ummmmmm! They smell good!"

Everyone ate the delicious hot dogs in rolls oozing with mustard and spicy relish, then started on plump, juicy hamburgers.

After lunch Bert, Harry, Freddie, and Ralph decided to take a walk in the woods to hunt for Indian arrow heads, which Captain McGinty said were plenteous on this lake. At the edge of the woods was a tree that interested Bert. "I'm sure that's an arrow head high in the trunk," he told himself.

As Harry and Freddie went on, he climbed up. Bert was right—he had seen an arrow head, but it was a modern one made of steel. No Indian had shot it there!

Bert pocketed the arrow and started down. As he happened to glance toward the *Blue-bird,* he blinked in amazement. For an instant a face had looked out from one of the portholes in the hold!

"But everybody's here on the island," Bert thought. "Was I seeing things?"

Deciding he had better mention it to his father, Bert shinned down the tree and hurried across the beach. Mr. Bobbsey thought it best to investigate at once, so the two went to the *Bluebird* in the dinghy. They searched every part of the houseboat but found no one.

"The face you thought you saw, Bert," his father said, "must have been made by a reflection from the water—an optical illusion."

"I suppose so," Bert agreed, but he continued to wonder about it.

He joined his companions, and the four boys each found an old arrow head. Proudly they displayed them to their parents and sisters.

After the families had a light snack for supper, they said good-by and went back to their houseboats. There was a period of quiet on board as everyone found books and magazines to read. The children sprawled on the deck or curled up in chairs with theirs.

Presently the warm peaceful evening was shattered by furious barking from Snap. What had bothered him?

The whole family went inside to find out. Snap was standing in the passageway between the galley and dining-playroom. He was growling and showing his teeth, as he did when he got in a dog fight.

"What's the matter, old fellow?" asked Bert. "Do you see something?"

Snap whirled around and looked at the children and their parents. Then he turned back and glared at one of the locker doors. With a loud bark, Snap sprang toward it, clawing at the wood with the sharp nails on his paws.

CHAPTER XV

FLOSSIE PLAYS DETECTIVE

"COME away, Snap!" Flossie ordered, pulling on her pet's collar.

But Snap did not obey his young mistress! Instead he kept clawing the locker, at the same time giving short, excited barks.

"Why don't we open the door and let Snap see what's in there?" suggested Nan.

"Good idea!" Mrs. Bobbsey said approvingly. "Maybe it's only a mouse."

"But suppose it's a rat," Dorothy spoke up. "Rats often live on boats. Maybe they've been taking the food."

"Sure, and drinking milk right out of a bottle," said Harry.

"Rats!" murmured Flossie. "Oo, I'm not going to stay here!" She dashed off.

"Well, we'll find out," said Mr. Bobbsey.

As he turned the latch, there was a noise inside the locker. It sounded as though something had been knocked down off a shelf.

Hearing this, Snap growled and sprang closer to the door, ready to jump inside the minute it was opened. But a second later, to everyone's surprise, they found that *the storage closet was empty!*

"Huh!" said Freddie in disgust and walked off.

Snap, disappointed, pawed around the floor of the closet, sticking his nose behind the boxes of canned

food. The big dog breathed heavily and wagged his tail, but there was nothing to catch.

"If it was a mouse or a rat, he sure got away," Bert said, looking carefully for signs of a small hole through which one might have escaped.

"Thank goodness!" exclaimed Dinah. "I don't want any rats near my galley!"

"I'll set a trap, to be on the safe side, Dad," said Bert, and he went to get some cheese from the refrigerator.

While the rest of the family drifted off to do other things, Bert hunted around and finally found an old mousetrap, which he baited with the cheese. He laid it on the locker floor.

Flossie was very tired from her day's adventure and went to bed very early. For this reason she awoke about five o'clock. As the little girl sat up to look out the window, she thought she heard someone crying.

"Who could that be?" Flossie thought, seeing it was not Nan or Dorothy. "Maybe I can help the person not to feel so sad."

She hopped out of her bunk and went into the corridor. First she stopped at the boys' door. The sobbing did not come from there. Next she listened at Mr. and Mrs. Bobbsey's cabin. Not a sound from within.

"Oh dear, it must be Dinah," Flossie thought. "Poor Dinah!"

But it was not Dinah either. Flossie stood still and listened to the muffled crying.

"There's only one person left," Flossie told herself. "Captain McGinty. But why would he be crying?"

As Flossie went to the deck and started to climb the steps to his quarters, she tried to picture the big, stern man shedding tears. Suddenly she stopped short. The man was not crying! Instead he was snoring very loudly. Flossie backed down the stairway.

She stood on deck, absently taking in the beautiful sunrise. The crying had ceased. Everything seemed lovely now. Suddenly Snoop appeared as if from nowhere, brushed against Flossie's ankles, and began to purr. The little girl patted him, saying, "Good morning, Snoop." Then the cat jumped to the rail.

Flossie had a thought. "Were you crying, Snoop?" she asked. "It must have been you. Are you sick?" The cat certainly looked fit, though, and Flossie shrugged, still puzzled by the mysterious soft sobbing.

The others on the houseboat were startled to hear Flossie's story. There were various guesses about the crying. Some agreed that it might have been Snoop, others, that Flossie might have heard someone in a rowboat.

"I'm sure it's nothing to worry about," said Mrs. Bobbsey.

At breakfast Captain McGinty said he would chart their course so the voyagers might see the beautiful waterfall at the end of Arrow Lake, as they had requested.

"It's called Arrow Falls, but why I don't know," he said. "I believe there's some strange Indian story connected with it."

"Maybe somebody there can tell us," said Nan, interested at once.

Mr. Bobbsey, too, vaguely recalled a story about the waterfall. "It hasn't been there a long while," he said. "The Indians made it for some reason."

"What was it?" Bert asked eagerly.

But his father could not remember. He and the captain promised to try to think of it, but as the day wore on, they were unable to do so. About noontime Captain McGinty moored the *Bluebird* at the town of Brighthaven to buy fuel and supplies.

Dinah had requested this. "What with my family's big appetites," she said, "and food disappearing, my shelves sure are empty."

Mrs. Bobbsey said all the children might go ashore with her and Mr. Bobbsey and have lunch. Eagerly they went down the gangplank. Brighthaven was a quaint town of old-fashioned stores and homes.

"Look!" said Nan presently. "All the buildings have dates over the front doors."

"They tell the year in which they were built," Mr. Bobbsey explained.

"I see a fish store," Freddie cried. "I'm going to buy a playmate for my goldfish."

The group went inside and looked over the display. Freddie finally decided on a fish he called Jet because a fin on top of its tail made the little boy think of an airplane. It was put into a box with water and Freddie proudly carried it away.

After Mrs. Bobbsey had made a lot of purchases at a market, she led her family to a restaurant which fascinated the children. The walls were covered with old-time guns and rifles, and in a showcase were figures dressed in Revolutionary War period costumes. The waitresses wore old-fashioned dresses and caps.

Suddenly Flossie asked, "Mother, is the food out-of-date, too?"

The others laughed and Mrs. Bobbsey said she hardly thought so. But the menu did consist of a good old-time kind of vegetable soup, chicken pie, and rice pudding.

After lunch the family strolled around a little park with a zoo in it. Mr. Bobbsey bought each of them a bag of peanuts and a banana, and the children enjoyed feeding them to the elephants and monkeys.

As Nan happened to look through one of the cages to another part of the park, she thought she saw a familiar figure. She grabbed her twin's arm.

"Bert!" Nan cried. "Look over there. Do you see what I see?" She pointed.

Her brother gazed ahead. "Why, it looks like Danny Rugg!" he exclaimed.

"I thought so too," said Nan, as the boy

whom she had been looking at disappeared in the crowd.

"Let's find out," Bert urged.

The twins excused themselves to the others and hurried off. They searched the park from one end to the other but could not find Danny.

"Do you suppose he saw us and ran off?" Nan asked.

"Probably. Well, we'd better get back."

They joined the others and did some more sightseeing, as well as inquiring about the story of Arrow Falls. But no one they questioned knew it.

Presently Flossie said, "I'm tired of looking. I want to go back to the boat and play."

"All right," her mother agreed.

The group ambled down the street and several minutes later reached the *Bluebird*. Stepping on the gangplank, the twins hailed Captain McGinty, who was leaning on the rail, to tell him of their afternoon's sightseeing.

Suddenly a wild, blood-curdling scream from inside the houseboat broke the serenity of the harbor.

"That sounded like Dinah!" Nan cried.

CHAPTER XVI

A TURNABOUT TRICK

BREAKING into a run, the Bobbseys hurried aboard the *Bluebird* and, with Captain Mc-Ginty, ran through the main cabin and down the main corridor to the galley.

Nan was the first to arrive. "What's the matter, Dinah?" she cried, staring at the cook in amazement.

Dinah was standing up on the counter, shaking all over. Her face was almost gray with fear as she looked at the galley floor.

Mice were scurrying about in every direction!

"Ugh!" Nan exclaimed, feeling a little squeamish herself.

The next instant the mice scooted out of the galley every which way to find hiding places. Some managed to hide themselves instantly, but the others scampered on into the various cabins.

By this time the houseboat was in an uproar. The men and boys were already trying to

Mice were scurrying in every direction!

catch the mice. Dorothy said she would help them. She grabbed a broom from the closet and started up the corridor.

"Oo-oo-oo!" Flossie screamed. "One's on my bunk!"

Dorothy cornered the mouse under the pillow and picked it up by its tail. As the little creature swung in the air, twisting and turning, Dorothy laughed at Flossie's horrified expression.

"He's a nice little mouse," she teased. "Wouldn't you like him for a playmate?"

"No, oh, no!" Flossie replied.

"Then I guess I'll have to throw him overboard," said Dorothy.

"Oh, please don't do that!" Flossie begged.

"Then what'll we do with him?"

Flossie thought for a minute, then said, "Let's take him up to a field and let him run away."

"Okay," said Dorothy. "We can put all the mice in a basket and take them out to some farm."

Harry, overhearing this, remarked, "I don't think the farmer will thank you, but we certainly can't keep these mice on board ship."

All this time Bert had been running around with a crab net, which he had once seen in the locker. With it he had managed to snare three of the mice. Mr. Bobbsey had caught two and the captain two.

"Are they all accounted for?" Nan asked.

No one knew, so they went to ask Dinah. She said she had counted twelve, so the search went on until finally the whole dozen mice were captured. They were then put into a covered basket, and the children went some distance down the shore and let them loose in a field.

Returning to the boat, they questioned Dinah as to where the mice had come from. Certainly, they had not been on board before the family had gone into Brighthaven.

Dinah said that she had been dusting the main cabin for a while. When she returned to the galley, she had noticed that the window was open wide. She remembered having closed it earlier because of the strong breeze. Starting toward the window, she had stumbled over a shoebox in the middle of the floor. The mice had jumped out.

The children looked at one another. Someone had deliberately brought the mice on board!

Bert looked out the window. Spotting something on the deck, he went outside and picked it up. "Look!" he said, returning with a penknife bearing the initials *D.R.*

"Danny Rugg!" cried Nan, and told the others of having seen Danny in the park. "I'll bet he climbed in through the galley window. Otherwise Dinah would have seen him."

Dinah said she did not see why the trick had been played on her. Bert was certain this had not been Danny's idea. The boy probably had intended to hide the mice in the children's cabins. But when Dinah had walked toward the galley, Danny had become frightened. He had left the shoebox on the floor and bolted out the window, losing the penknife in his haste.

"Harry," Bert said, "what do you say we go find Danny Rugg and play a trick on him?"

His cousin thought this was a good idea and said, "What could we do?"

Bert replied that he had noticed a shop in town which sold toy mechanical mice. They would get a couple of them and then search for Danny.

As they were about to leave the boat, Captain McGinty called:

"Hey, mates! Don't forget the sailboat races! They'll start in half an hour."

He referred to an annual racing event held by boat owners in the vicinity, and suggested the boys get back in time to watch the race. The boats would pass fairly close to the *Bluebird*.

"Wouldn't miss it," said Bert.

He and Harry hurried up to the main street of Brighthaven and made their purchase. Then they looked all around town for Danny, but could not find him. When the half hour was nearly up, the two boys decided to return to the shore so they would not miss seeing the sailboat race. By this time the waterfront was lined with people.

And standing in the crowd was Danny Rugg!

The race had not yet started, so Bert and Harry quietly made their way among the people until they were standing directly behind Danny. The bully was watching the sailboats so intently that he did not hear them come up. Bert winked at Harry and each boy took a toy mouse from his pocket and wound it up.

Bert winked again and dropped one mouse down Danny's shirt. At the same moment, Harry put the other in the boy's trouser pocket.

No one in the crowd had seen the two boys do this and they moved back a few feet. By now the fun had begun—Danny started to dance around, yelling at the top of his voice, "A spider! There's a spider down my back! It's stinging me! I'll be poisoned!"

At the same moment he noticed the wriggling in his pocket. Without thinking he put his hand in and touched the squirming object. He withdrew his hand and yelled even louder.

By this time a man who was standing near him exclaimed, "Take off your shirt!"

Danny tore it off and the mechanical mouse

dropped to the ground. It still kept wriggling in circles. Danny looked at it stupefied, then took the other toy from his pocket.

He suddenly became aware of a great guffawing not far away. He looked up just in time to see Bert and Harry hurrying away. Danny shook his fist at them. "I'll get you for this," he cried.

Bert and his cousin climbed aboard the *Bluebird* just as the sailboat race got under way. How exciting and how colorful it was! The turn around the bobbing marker at the side of the lake was not far from the houseboat. Its passengers cheered and clapped the racers on.

"I want that one with the red sails to win!" cried Freddie.

A few minutes later, his father said, "Well, I guess your wish is coming true. There goes the boat with the red sails over the finish line!"

After the race was over, Dorothy asked the boys how they had made out with their mouse joke. Everyone laughed heartily on hearing how they had gotten square with Danny.

"But watch your step, everybody," Bert warned. "He said he'd get even with us."

Freddie was not worried by this at all. In fact he wanted to take his little sailboat, *Duck-A-Way,* and play with it on the water. Mrs. Bobbsey asked Nan and Dorothy to go with the small twins up the shore a short way and watch Freddie and Flossie.

The four children quickly put on bathing suits and started out. There was enough breeze so that the attractive toy boat made very good speed. Freddie would let it go, and when it reached Flossie, who was farther up the beach, she would wade back with it to her brother. After a while they changed places.

"Well," said Nan presently, "have you had enough sailing?"

Freddie begged to let his boat make one more trip and Nan consented. The graceful toy was about halfway to the end of its voyage when without warning a heavy log came sailing through the air.

It landed square on the *Duck-A-Way* with a crash!

CHAPTER XVII

A SEA-BISCUIT YARN

WHEN Bert and Harry saw the log crash into Freddie's toy sailboat, they hurried up the shore. Quickly the boys looked in the opposite direction to see who had thrown the log.

They were just in time to catch a glimpse of Danny Rugg running off!

"He can't get away with this!" Harry cried, as Danny disappeared into a little woods.

"You help Freddie," Bert said. "I'll go after Danny!"

Bert raced off among the trees. He could see Danny running quickly toward the other end of the woods. Like a deer, Bert leaped after him. In a few minutes he caught up to the bully, grabbed him by his shirt, and swung him around.

"If you want to be mean, why don't you pick on somebody your own age?" Bert yelled.

"I'll do as I please," Danny answered defiantly and, drawing back his arm, aimed a blow at Bert's head.

The Bobbsey boy dodged and came back at Danny with a right uppercut. It landed square under Danny's chin and he reeled backward. But he recovered himself instantly and, scowling angrily, went at Bert with both fists. Bert retaliated with lightning-like thrusts.

Danny realized he was not getting the better of his opponent. He suddenly brought up one knee, caught Bert in the ribs, and swung him off balance. Down he went!

Danny was on top of him in a second, but before he had a chance to pin Bert down, the Bobbsey boy began to roll. The two went over and over, with arms and legs flying. First one got in a good punch, then the other.

"Hey, what's going on here?" a voice cried.

Both boys looked up to see a farmer standing near by. "Cut that out!" he ordered. "I don't want anybody getting hurt on my property!"

Instantly Bert and Danny got up. But Danny was not ready to stop fighting. He socked Bert hard on the cheek.

"Well, I call that dirty fighting!" said the farmer. "Hitting somebody when he isn't defending himself. Now you get out of here!" He glared at Danny.

Under the man's stern gaze, the troublesome

boy lost his air of defiance and slunk off. For the first time Bert noticed that the bully's nose was bleeding. Bert must have given him a harder punch than he had realized! He apologized to the farmer and then went off himself.

Back at the shore, Harry had rescued Freddie's toy sailboat. The *Duck-A-Way* had a gaping hole in the side and the mainsail was torn. Freddie looked very sad.

"Never mind," Nan was saying, "we'll fix it up somehow or get you a new one."

This made Freddie feel better. As Bert joined the group, everyone noticed his reddened cheeks, and asked, "What happened?"

Bert told of fighting Danny for having ruined the little sailboat. Freddie beamed and said, "That's swell. Thanks a lot, Bert."

The children walked back to the *Bluebird,* and soon Dinah had supper almost ready. Nan was in the kitchen helping her. As the cook opened the refrigerator to take out milk for the children, she gave a loud gasp.

"How much milk did you buy uptown, Nan?" she asked with a worried look.

"Eight quarts," Nan replied. "You said we still had two. Why—isn't there enough, Dinah?"

"There are only eight quarts of milk in the 'frigerator right this minute!" Dinah said emphatically. "Somebody took the other two!"

Nan looked thoughtful for a moment, then smiled. "Well, one person we can't blame this time," she said, "is the captain."

"That's right," Dinah agreed. "He was in town, too, and didn't come back till just before you all did."

After a little more discussion, Nan and Dinah decided that it must have been Danny Rugg who had taken the milk when he came aboard with the mice. This might be another reason he had not had time to go further with his joke.

At supper Captain McGinty said he had met a man down the shore that afternoon who knew all about the history of the Arrow Lake region. "Would you like to walk down there after a spell and talk to him?" he asked the children.

"Oh, yes!" they chorused.

As soon as they had finished eating, the little group set off. The man they were going to call on lived in a small fishing shack. He caught lake trout and sold them for a living.

Hearing his visitors arriving, the old man came outside his shack. He was a rather large man with a ruddy complexion, snow-white hair, and a beard. His eyes twinkled merrily as he drawled:

"Well, old Benny the trout man doesn't often

have so many visitors. Welcome! Will you come inside?"

The children were intrigued by the interior of the fishing shack. All kinds of fishing rods stood about the room, and the walls were lined with glassed-in boxes of fishing flies. When Bert mentioned these, Benny said he had made them himself and that, years before, he used to sell them.

"This here is one of my specials," he explained. "I call it my Jet Bug." Bert laughed and said it looked ex-

actly like a speedy insect and must certainly fool the fish. Benny's eyes twinkled and he nodded.

Harry was particularly interested in a very long, heavy pole that stood in one corner of the room. "Isn't this a pretty big rod for lake fishing?" he asked.

"Oh, I didn't always fish in lakes," replied Benny. "Some years ago I was a deep-sea fisherman. That pole brought me in many a tuna, and once I got a shark on it."

At this remark, Freddie's eyes opened very wide. "A shark?" he said. "You mean those big fish with awful sharp teeth?"

Benny said this was exactly what he meant, and that he had had a hard tussle with the old fellow. "But I won the battle," he added, grinning. "If you'll turn around, you'll see him there on the wall."

The shark was mounted on a plaque. But even in this harmless state, it looked very fierce and unfriendly. Flossie shivered and remarked she was glad there were no such fish swimming in Arrow Lake!

Captain McGinty now spoke up and said the children were interested in hearing the history of the lake and Arrow Falls. The friendly fisherman smiled, invited everyone to sit down, and went to a shelf for a large tin box. He took off the lid and said:

"I never tell yarns unless my listeners are eating sea biscuits."

His callers looked at one another. They certainly wanted to hear the legend of the lake, but they did not know if they would care for sea biscuits. Seeing their worried faces, Benny laughed heartily and said they need not worry.

"These are very special," he said, passing the box to Nan. "Try one and tell the rest what it tastes like."

Nan took the large white cracker in her hand and bit off a small piece. Then she began to laugh. "It's good," she said. "Sort of a combination candy and cracker. It's delicious."

Benny passed the box around, and after everyone was nibbling on the biscuits, he put the tin back on the shelf. Then he sat down on a stool facing his audience.

"Arrow Lake," he began his story, "wasn't always called that. Years and years ago, Indians lived here. They had a famous good-luck golden arrow. But it disappeared, and after that the tribe had bad luck. The arrow has never been found.

"Meanwhile, the lake was named after it, and there's an old legend that whoever discovers it will have good luck the rest of his life."

As Benny paused, Nan spoke up excitedly, "Maybe someone could find the arrow now, if it wasn't destroyed."

"No," Benny replied, "I don't believe it was." He looked at them and smiled. "Who knows— even you children may find the valuable golden arrow!"

CHAPTER XVIII

INDIAN GHOSTS

"I WANT to find the golden arrow!" Freddie shouted, jumping up and going over to Benny, the trout catcher.

"Well, I hope you do, son," said the fisherman. He went on to say that what had happened in connection with the Indians' golden arrow seemed to have changed the whole water system of Arrow Lake.

"Not many natives lived around here at that time," Benny explained. "Suddenly one year they found that a stream which formerly ran into the lake had somehow been diverted, making a great waterfall. After folks heard about the missing golden arrow, they named it Arrow Falls."

"You mean somebody *made* the falls?" Freddie asked.

"No one knows for sure," the old fisherman said. "But most folks think it wasn't the work of nature—that some of the Indians did it. But why, is a mystery."

As the old man paused, Bert said, "Please tell us the rest of the legend."

Benny related that once a powerful tribe of Indians had lived at the end of the lake near Lemby Creek. It was ruled by Chief Eagle, a fierce, cunning warrior. He had subdued various smaller tribes and was in command of a large section.

"He ruled his tribe firmly," the fisherman went on. "His son, Ko-sa-mia, meaning White Horse, was of a gentler nature and did not always see eye to eye with his father. Ko-sa-mia loved the animals in the forest, and the people too, and did not want to be making war all the time."

"I like him," said Flossie suddenly.

"Of course, Ko-sa-mia was being trained by his father to rule the tribe. He had pledged him to marry a chief's daughter of another tribe. But Ko-sa-mia did not love this Indian maiden and felt that his father had arranged the marriage only to be able to rule the other tribe.

"Ko-sa-mia, who was a handsome young brave, had fallen in love with the daughter of the Medicine Man of his own tribe. Her name was White Fawn. She was very pretty and had gentle, sweet eyes. She also loved the animals in the forest, and, from the time they were small children, she and Ko-sa-mia had played together. They had tamed wild dog puppies and had several pet fawns.

"Well, it was getting near Ko-sa-mia's eighteenth birthday. That was the time his father had chosen for the wedding. Ko-sa-mia had begged his father to change his mind and let him marry White Fawn, but the chief was determined to have his way. Then, the morning of the wedding, something surprising happened. Ko-sa-mia and White Fawn disappeared!"

"I'm glad they did," said Dorothy. "Did they get married and live happily ever after?"

Old Benny said he supposed so, but no one in their tribe ever saw them again.

"And here's where the story of the golden arrow comes in," he continued. "When Ko-sa-mia disappeared, he took the arrow with him. Actually it had been given to him by his father when he was a little boy. But the tribe had come to feel that it was a good-luck symbol which belonged to them all."

Benny shook his head thoughtfully. "It certainly seemed to be true," he said, "because after Ko-sa-mia vanished, everything began to go wrong for Chief Eagle's tribe. First, their crops did not grow well, then sickness came to the tribe.

"A good many of the Indians thought that misfortune had come to them because Chief

Eagle had refused to listen to his son. The chief was so angry that he had decreed that Ko-sa-mia and White Fawn could never return to the tribe. And they never did!"

"It served him right," said Flossie, tossing her curls. "Is that the end of the story?"

"Well, practically," said the old fisherman, "except there's a good ending. Years later, a handsome young brave visited the new chief who was then ruling the tribe. He introduced himself as Straight Arrow, the son of Ko-sa-mia and White Fawn. He said his parents had died, but before their deaths they had asked him to visit their old tribe.

"Straight Arrow claimed his parents had sworn him to secrecy as to where they had lived. Then the young man had ended his visit, saying he had no desire to become ruler of the tribe. He now lived out West and was head of a large school for Indian children. He loved his work and did not want to be an Indian chief."

As Benny finished his story, Bert asked, "Didn't Straight Arrow have the golden arrow?"

"No, he didn't. And when the folks of the tribe asked him about it, he said he had never seen it."

"Is Straight Arrow still alive?" Nan asked.

Benny said that the Indian had died years

ago, without telling any of the secrets he probably had learned from his mother and father.

"So the mystery of the golden arrow is still unsolved," he said. Then Benny chuckled. "Some of the folks around here say that the ghosts of Ko-sa-mia and White Fawn haunt Arrow Lake. Also, that on bright moonlight nights, you can see them dancing in the water at the top of Arrow Falls."

"And they don't get drowned?" asked Flossie, to whom the story was very real.

Benny chuckled. "It's just a yarn, my child. I daresay that the way the moonlight plays on the water makes it look as if figures were dancing there."

"I see," said Flossie.

But the instant she and the others returned to the *Bluebird,* she ran to tell Dinah the whole story. The good-natured cook chuckled and her big eyes rolled. When Flossie finished her story, Dinah said:

"Well, I guess that's what we got aboard this here *Bluebird*—Indian ghosts! They must be the ones who've been takin' our food!"

Nan, who had been standing in the doorway of the galley listening, began to laugh. "But ghosts don't eat," she said.

"I don't care!" Dinah retorted. "Somebody's been takin' food out of my 'frigerator an' my breadbox. If there's nobody on this here houseboat that's been takin' it, it must be a ghost!"

"I think," said Nan with a twinkle, "that your ghost will turn out to be a very big man with a very big appetite."

"Maybe so, maybe so," Dinah said and resumed her work.

Early the next morning Captain McGinty said they would go on to Arrow Falls. Bert and Harry followed the skipper to the wheelhouse and asked if they might take turns steering the houseboat.

"All right, mates," the captain said. "Keep the shore to starboard."

Harry took over first, then, about a mile farther up the lake, he suddenly turned to Bert.

"Gosh! I forgot that I promised Dorothy I'd teach her some more about the short-wave set. Will you take over, Bert?"

"Sure!" his cousin said happily, relieving him at the wheel.

Bert enjoyed being helmsman. He seemed to understand the running of the boat so well that a little while later the captain said to him:

"Bert, I want to speak to your father for a minute. Would you mind staying up here alone?"

"Not at all," the boy answered.

"Call me immediately if you catch sight of the spinning wheel!" the captain ordered, going out the door.

"Aye, aye, sir!" said Bert.

After the man had gone, Bert began to wonder what the spinning wheel was. But he had little time to think about it. Going around a sharp bend in the lake, Bert suddenly saw a strange and terrifying sight. He had permitted the houseboat to come too close to the shore. Now it seemed as if there was nothing ahead but rocks!

Bert pulled the wheel hard to the left, trying to run out toward the middle of the lake, but he was too late. The houseboat was caught in a strong current that ran between the jagged rocks.

There was no time to call Captain McGinty for help. "I'll have to do it myself!" Bert thought frantically.

As he tried to hold the wheel firm to guide the houseboat through the current and away from the rocks, the boy held his breath.

Would he have the skill to steer the *Bluebird* through the narrow, dangerous passageway?

CHAPTER XIX

A MEAN ACCUSATION

FOR a second Bert Bobbsey feared that he could not steer the *Bluebird* through the strong current without the houseboat crashing against the rocks. Then fresh strength seemed to come to the boy. Tensely he gripped the wheel.

"Now left!" he told himself. "Now right!"

The rushing current added to the speed of the *Bluebird,* so she was going much faster than usual. Bert knew the rocks would tear a gaping hole in the boat if it hit one.

"I've just got to hold the course straight!" the boy thought grimly.

A second later the wheel twisted and was almost wrenched from his hands. But, with lightning speed, he yanked it back in time, avoiding an accident.

The *Bluebird* now began to pitch, and once Bert thought he heard her scrape against some rocks. But she went on, apparently without any damage being done.

"There's not much more to go!" Bert assured himself. "If I can only—"

Suddenly the boy saw a terrifying sight.

Directly ahead of him was a whirlpool! And as Bert looked at it, the swirling waters suddenly rose into the air, almost in front of the *Bluebird!*

For an instant Bert closed his eyes, fully expecting that the houseboat would be sucked into the whirling geyser and dashed to bits. But as he opened them, Bert suddenly realized that to the left, or portside, there were no more rocks.

There was still time for him to save the houseboat!

Using every ounce of strength in his arms, Bert yanked the wheel hard to the left. By inches he kept the *Bluebird* away from the swirling column of water. But could he hold it there?

At this moment the door of the wheelhouse flew open and Captain McGinty rushed in. He was panting heavily from running up the stairs.

"Thank goodness you've come!" Bert gasped.

As the captain reached the boy's side, he started to lift his hands from the wheel, but the captain yelled, "It'll take both of us to keep out of that spinning wheel!"

The houseboat groaned as if she objected. But within a few seconds the *Bluebird* was out of danger and sailing in calm water!

"Good work, mate!" said Captain Mc-Ginty, slapping Bert on the back.

"You were really the one who pulled us out," Bert said shakily.

"Nothing of the sort, nothing of the sort," the officer declared. "You stuck to the wheel through the worst of it—like a true first mate should."

By this time Mr. Bobbsey, the other members of the family, and even Dinah were crowding the stairway to the wheelhouse and calling up to Bert. He was loudly praised and Flossie declared he was the "life-savingest" brother anybody could have.

Bert suddenly grinned. "Anyhow, I know what a 'spinning wheel' is. That whirlpool sure looked like one!"

Captain McGinty had pulled a chart from a cubbyhole in the wheelhouse. He studied it carefully, then said, "Um. The swift current and 'spinning wheel' are marked for about a mile farther down the lake."

"What causes them?" Bert asked.

"An underground stream running into the lake. I certainly wouldn't have left you, Bert, if I'd had any idea we were this close. We had a lucky escape and should be thankful."

"Praise be!" came Dinah's voice.

Mrs. Bobbsey, who had been very disturbed during the harrowing experience, said that Dinah spoke for them all. She hoped they would be able to go on to Arrow Falls without further dangerous incidents.

"According to the chart," said the captain, "there'll be only smooth sailing ahead. But I won't leave this wheelhouse for a moment while we're moving."

Suddenly Harry said that just before the excitement, he had contacted a friend of Bert's in Lakeport named Bob Jones, who had a short-wave set. "Bob was just about to give me an important message. He's been standing by a good while. I'd better go back and talk to him."

Bert went along and in a few minutes Harry had contacted Bob again. All of a sudden Harry frowned and looked concerned. He listened carefully to the message coming in.

"Tell Mr. Bobbsey that Sam has been trying to get in touch with him. It seems some boy ran away from home and his stepfather is blaming Mr. Bobbsey."

Bert jumped across the room to listen more closely. He asked Harry to switch on the sending set and ask Bob what the man's name was. Harry did so and the answer came back, "Hardman."

Harry now asked for more details and was told that Mr. Hardman had gone to the Bobbsey home. He had said he was going to have the twins' father arrested for helping his son leave the farm. He had looked everywhere for the boy and had not been able to find him.

Bert was stunned. Without waiting to hear any more, he dashed from the Communications Shack and went to speak to his father and mother, who were on deck.

"I can hardly believe such a thing," said Mr. Bobbsey, after his son told him of Mr. Hardman's accusation.

"You aren't going to pay any attention to it, of course, are you?" Mrs. Bobbsey spoke up. "How could that man tell such an untruth?"

Mr. Bobbsey was thoughtful for several seconds, then said, "I might have a hard time disproving Mr. Hardman's claim. Bruce disappeared soon after my telling his stepfather I would have him reported for cruelty to the boy. It certainly looks bad for me."

"What will you do, Dad?" Bert asked.

Mr. Bobbsey said they would have to tie up at the nearest town and he would telephone home to get more details from Sam. Then he would call Mr. Hardman and if he made no headway with the man, he would get in touch with his lawyer and have him talk to the farmer.

"But I'm afraid Mr. Hardman will be a difficult customer to deal with," Mr. Bobbsey observed wryly.

There was a small town about a mile ahead and the *Bluebird* was turned in that direction. The houseboat was secured and Mr. Bobbsey at once went to a telephone booth on the dock to put in the calls. His family waited anxiously to hear the outcome of his conversations. When he returned to the *Bluebird,* they could see that he was upset.

"Mr. Hardman is a scoundrel," the twins' father declared angrily. "Not one of his accusations is true. Some day I'm going to make that man eat his words!"

Mrs. Bobbsey laid a hand on her husband's arm. "Richard," she said gently, "since Mr. Hardman's statements are ridiculous, please try to forget them. Remember, you're on a vacation, getting a rest, and I don't want anything to spoil the trip for you."

"You're right," Mr. Bobbsey conceded, and smiled at his family. "Sam says that the police have found no clues as to where Bruce is."

"I still think he's trying to find his uncle," Bert spoke up, "and hasn't notified Mr. Hardman of his whereabouts."

Mrs. Bobbsey said she felt that the boy would not have run away from home unless he had a pretty good idea where he was headed. He would not dare go aimlessly from place to place, or the police surely would have picked him up.

Suddenly Flossie gave a tremendous sigh. "Oh dear," she said. "I wish I knew where Bruce is. Maybe he's cold and hungry."

"I do, too," said Nan.

Presently the *Bluebird* shoved off. Everyone tried to be cheerful, and the subject of Mr. Hardman's accusations was not brought up again. But secretly everyone was worried. It was a serious thing to be falsely blamed for causing a young boy's disappearance!

It was late afternoon before the passengers aboard the *Bluebird* came in sight of Arrow Falls. The sunlight, playing on the water, made a perfect rainbow.

"Oh, isn't it bee-yoo-ti-full!" Flossie exclaimed, clapping her hands.

Mrs. Bobbsey brought a camera and took several pictures. Dorothy and Harry, who had never seen such a waterfall, were intrigued, declaring it was one of the most lovely sights they had ever witnessed. The top of the falls, crowned by the blue of the sky and billowy white clouds, was about seventy-five feet above the surface of the lake.

The water fell from a ledge of rock, surrounded on two sides by trees in various shades of green. The water cascaded into a basin below, sending up a white mist of spray.

"I want to try the bouncing-balls trick!" cried Freddie. He ran to his cabin and took some small rubber balls from his suitcase.

The *Bluebird* was anchored in the cove near Arrow Falls, but not close enough to be disturbed by any strong currents of water.

"Please, may we go out in the rubber boats right away?" Freddie asked his mother.

"Yes, but you mustn't go too near the falls."

The children promised and quickly donned their bathing suits. Eagerly they put the life-boats over the side of the *Bluebird* and one by one went down the ladder.

Snap stood on deck, giving a series of short barks. "Oh, he wants to go with us," said Flossie.

"Come on, fellow!" called Bert. "Jump!"

The dog leaped into the boy's arms. The children sat down and paddled nearer the falls to get a close-up view. Then they went ashore.

"I'm going to throw the first ball," Freddie announced, and tossed one of the rubber balls directly into the waterfall.

It danced in the spray for several seconds until it reached a certain point. Then the ball was forced down, disappearing under the water. The children watched eagerly until it came to the surface a good distance away. Slowly the ball began to float toward the shore.

For several minutes all the children had fun throwing balls. Snap barked excitedly, then suddenly dashed into the water and began to swim toward the waterfall.

"Come back, Snap!" Bert commanded.

Flossie, who had thought her pet was going after one of the balls, began to giggle. She said, "Look! Snap's going to take a waterfall bath!"

"Snap, come back here!" Bert called again.

But the dog paid no attention. He was getting closer and closer to the tumbling water.

"Stop him!" Freddie cried, worried.

Suddenly Snap's head disappeared underneath the water. For a brief instant the children saw the tip of his tail sticking up in a pool of foam. Then that, too, went under.

Breathlessly the Bobbseys and their cousins waited, hoping for a glimpse of Snap some distance away where the balls had reappeared. But their pet did not come to the surface.

"Oh!" Flossie screamed. "Maybe poor Snap's drowned!"

CHAPTER XX

ARROW FALLS' SECRET

WITH the thought that their beloved dog was gone, Flossie burst into tears. Nan's throat was choked and the other children looked very sober.

Suddenly Bert said, "Maybe I can find Snap and save him!" He slid into the water and started swimming toward the falls.

"Oh, be careful!" Nan shouted. "That's terribly dangerous!"

The noise of the thundering water kept Bert from hearing her, and he plowed on. Freddie could not bear to watch and, turning around, looked upward. He gasped in surprise, then pointed to a rock ledge at one side of the top of the waterfall.

"Snap's not lost!" the little boy cried out excitedly. "There he is!"

"Where?" asked the others, amazed.

"Up there!" Freddie said. "See?"

Snap was vigorously shaking water from his coat. Seeing the children below, he gave a happy bark and wagged his tail.

"Well I'll be a kangaroo's pocket!" Harry exclaimed. "How did Snap get up there?"

"I can't imagine," Dorothy replied, looking thoughtfully at the distance between the place where Snap had disappeared and the spot where he was now standing. "He must have flown up to the top!"

After heaving a sigh of relief, Nan at once thought of her twin. Bert had almost reached the dangerous area of the cascading water.

"Come on, let's all shout to Bert and make him come back!" she ordered.

Together the children made megaphones of their hands and called to Bert with all their might. Finally he turned his head, and the others pointed to the ledge above. Seeing Snap, the boy grinned and swung around to swim back.

At this moment Flossie called out, "Oh, Snap's going to slip and fall!" She covered her eyes as the Bobbseys' pet jumped to another ledge.

"Snap's as sure-footed as a mountain goat," Dorothy assured her small cousin, who opened one eye a little. Nevertheless, Dorothy yelled up to the animal, "Come down, Snap!"

But the dog paid no attention to the order, and as soon as Bert came ashore the children decided to go up and get him. After searching for a stout stick, in case they should encounter a snake on the wooded hill, the group started its upward climb.

Bert and Harry, who were used to difficult outdoor hiking, cautioned the others to make sure of always putting their feet down on firm ground. Halfway up the steep hill, they found the going easier. There were more trees to grasp and fewer loose rocks over which to stumble.

Finally reaching the top, the children looked around with interest. A mountain stream cut through the woods and emptied into the falls. A jagged rock formation bordered the falls on both sides, stretching ten feet in height.

Snap rushed over to meet the children, and at once Flossie and Freddie hugged their pet lovingly. But Flossie scolded him. "You were a naughty dog to go off by yourself, Snap."

"Anyhow, he gave us an excuse to come up and investigate," Bert replied. "Come on, Harry, let's see how he got up here. Snap, go to it!"

The dog broke away from the small twins and darted ahead. Running across the rocks, he suddenly turned left and disappeared behind a boulder.

"Quick!" shouted Freddie. "Don't let Snap get away again!"

Reaching the spot where the dog had disappeared, the children looked down in amazement. Snap's head was poking through a narrow crevice, which was part of a larger opening. This was covered by a large rock.

Bert, Harry, and the two older girls pushed and heaved at the rock with all their strength. Finally it toppled to one side and the children stared into a sloping, dark passageway.

"Well I'll be—it's a cave!" Bert exclaimed. "I wonder if this is Snap's secret!"

Snap was barking continuously somewhere ahead. The children heard the clicking of his paws. It seemed as if the dog were walking down some steps, for the noise grew fainter.

"Maybe this is the opening to some sort of a tunnel!" Harry suggested excitedly.

"I'm going to the *Bluebird* for flashlights," Bert announced. "I'll see if Mother and Dad and Captain McGinty want to help solve this mystery with us!"

As Bert left, Snap emerged from the cave holding something in his mouth. "Give that to me, Snap!" Flossie commanded. "You'll get cave germs!"

Snap obeyed Flossie, dropping an object that resembled a stick. Harry picked it up curiously and suddenly exclaimed:

"Why this is a pipe! It's shaped like an Indian peace pipe I once saw in a museum."

Freddie danced around happily, pretending

he was a wild Indian and making warlike noises. "Wha! *Wha—whooo!*" he cried.

Remembering the Indian legend which Benny the troutman had told them, the children were eager to explore and were delighted when Bert returned. Mr. and Mrs. Bobbsey and the captain had followed him in the dinghy, carrying several flashlights.

Flossie quickly showed the grownups the pipe, which they agreed certainly looked like an Indian relic. Then Bert switched on a powerful flashlight and everyone peered into the opening.

"Hm!" the captain exclaimed.

A few feet ahead, an uneven stairway carved out of rock led downward. The excited group crowded in to look at it.

Snap ran down the steps quickly and Harry shouted, "Let's follow him!"

Everyone lighted their flashes and the group started down the steps cautiously, taking care not to step on any loose rocks. Mr. Bobbsey and the boys went first. The ceiling over the stairway was high enough for even the tall captain to walk under without stooping.

"This is spooky!" Flossie exclaimed, holding her mother's hand tightly as she looked at the weird shadows the lights made on the jagged rocks.

Finally they reached the bottom of the

rough-hewn stairway and stepped into a large
chamber. It was damp, and moss-covered rocks
lined the three stone walls. The fourth wall of
the room was an arch of stone with a small
opening to the floor like a doorway. Beyond it
thundered the falls.

"Gee! A water door!" said Freddie loudly,
wanting to be heard over the noise of the water.

"So this is how Snap got to the top of Arrow
Falls!" Bert exclaimed. "He swam underwater
and ended up in this room!"

Captain McGinty chuckled. "It's one of the
strangest sights I've ever seen. Your pet is a
mighty smart dog!"

"I wonder where Snap found the Indian
pipe?" Dorothy mused.

"Chances are that some Indians lived in this
cave once," the captain guessed.

"You mean Ko-sa-mia and White Fawn?"
Nan asked quickly.

"It could be."

"And before they died," said Nan excitedly,
"they changed the course of a river and made
it run this way so there'd be a waterfall."

"But why?" asked Flossie.

"To hide the cave and all their treasures!"
said Nan.

"Let's hunt for them!" Bert urged.

At this moment Snap barked and ran across
the rocky room. Bert followed his movements

with the flashlight, wondering what the dog was after. Snap started to dig in the moist ground furiously and the others grew excited. But after several minutes their pet stood up and stretched, displaying a big, empty hole!

"Snap just wanted to play," Freddie said, disappointed. "Or maybe he heard the Indian ghosts Benny told us about!"

"Sh!" said Dorothy. "You know that's silly."

Everyone started searching in earnest. The large flashlight was set in the middle of the room and the smaller ones were used by the explorers to peer into crevices.

Nan, leaning against a rocky ledge to rest a moment, suddenly felt something move. Her arm had dislodged a rock in back of her! She jumped aside quickly as the rock crashed to the floor.

Her companions turned quickly, afraid someone had been injured, then relaxed. In a moment Nan stepped to the opening left by the falling rock and directed her light inside. Seeing something unusual, she called the others to come.

"Look at this!"

Running to Nan's side, everyone gaped in wonder. Inside a niche stood an assortment of beautifully decorated pottery jugs and bowls; copper knives and utensils; seashell jewelry and wampum. All were remarkably well preserved.

Nan directed her light inside the opening

"The treasure!" Nan cried. "Ko-sa-mia's treasure!"

Of course, there was nothing to prove this, and Mr. Bobbsey said they would take the articles to the museum in Brighthaven for examination.

Nan lifted the pieces out carefully, handing them one by one to her parents and the others. Flossie put on a necklace and Freddie proudly carried a small knife.

As Nan felt in the back of the niche for the last piece, her fingers touched something sharp. She gingerly drew it out. The article was covered with what seemed to be a piece of animal hide, now tender from age.

"What could this be?" Nan asked. "Something especially important, I guess."

"Open it!" Dorothy said excitedly.

The children held their lights closer, as Nan peeled off the covering.

"A golden arrow!" cried Bert. "Ko-sa-mia's golden arrow!"

"I believe you're right!" Captain McGinty exclaimed. "But I never thought you'd find it."

He suggested that they return to the *Bluebird* now where they could look over their findings more carefully.

Eagerly they climbed back up the stairway, then descended to the spot where the lifeboats and dinghy had been beached.

The various pieces were carefully placed in the bottom of the dinghy, into which the grownups stepped. But Freddie would not part with his copper knife and got into one of the rubber boats, clutching it tightly in his hands. Flossie kept the necklace.

The twins and their cousins chattered excitedly about the Indian legend and the treasures which had been hidden in the cavern. The dinghy reached the houseboat first, and the grownups went aboard. The boys were next.

"You're slow!" Freddie called down to the girls, who were still some distance away.

Only Flossie looked up. The next moment she cried out, "Bruce! Bruce Watson! What are you doing in there?"

Instantly Nan and Dorothy looked up to where the little girl was pointing at a porthole.

"You're dreaming," said Dorothy. "Nobody's there."

"I am not!" Flossie insisted.

In her excitement the little girl had risen and was jumping up and down.

"Cut that out!" cried Dorothy.

But Flossie had already leaned over too far, while staring at the porthole. She teetered from one side to the other and suddenly fell forward.

Splash!

CHAPTER XXI

A STRANGE NIGHT

"WELL, FLOSSIE," said Dorothy, helping her small cousin back into the lifeboat, "you're really having your troubles. Seeing ghosts and falling overboard—"

"I didn't see a ghost. I saw Bruce," Flossie declared stoutly.

Nan and Dorothy looked at the little girl tolerantly, but when Bert heard the story he began to wonder. He recalled the face he thought he had seen in the porthole while the Bobbseys were on Tomahawk Island.

"But where could Bruce be hiding on the boat?" thought Bert. "We've searched everywhere."

Suddenly Bert decided on something different than a search. He would try calling the boy's name. Walking from place to place, he said loudly:

"Hi, Bruce! Bruce Watson! We know you're aboard! Come on out!"

But there was no answer, and finally Bert

concluded that he and Flossie had been mistaken. Everyone agreed with him except Flossie herself. The little girl was disappointed that Freddie did not side with her—this was the first time she could remember that her twin had failed to back her up.

Flossie decided to go to bed soon after supper and think the whole thing over. Freddie, missing her, guessed the reason. He had begun to think that there might be something to her idea after all.

Quietly he went to his twin's cabin. Flossie was sitting up in her bunk, staring out the window.

"I thought you might be asleep, Flossie," he said in an unusually quiet voice.

"No. I'm wondering about Bruce Watson," she replied, motioning her brother to sit down on her bunk. "I just know he's on board this houseboat, Freddie."

"That's why I came to see you," Freddie announced. "I think he's on board, too!"

Flossie hugged her twin happily. "You're the first one who believes me!" she cried.

The little twins talked things over and finally decided that they would make a search later that night, when everyone else was asleep.

"We'll start with the locker where Snap acted funny once," said Freddie.

After winding up the girls' clock, which had

a luminous dial, Freddie made sure it was the same time as the clock in the boys' cabin.

"You keep awake until midnight," he said. "Then sneak out of the room real quiet and meet me at the storage locker."

"Okay!" said Flossie, who was eager to begin the search. She nestled back in her bunk and Freddie left the room to join the other children on deck.

Captain McGinty was pointing out various small stars to the older children and Harry was saying, "I can hardly wait to take a trip to the moon."

"I'd like to go to Mars," said Bert.

Freddie listened a moment, then he kissed his parents good night. He went into the main cabin for two flashlights and hurried off to his own quarters.

Fifteen minutes later Bert and Harry decided to retire. They bade the captain and the others good night and headed inside.

"You're not asleep, Freddie?" Bert asked, as they entered the cabin.

"Not yet," Freddie replied, quickly hiding the two flashlights underneath his pillow.

It seemed to Freddie that the older boys took an extra long time getting ready for bed. Even after the lights were out, Bert and Harry discussed the day's events again. They were still wondering why the hidden cave behind the waterfall had not been discovered by anyone else.

"You awake, Freddie?" Bert asked, for the little fellow had had nothing to say for several minutes.

Silence! Freddie was pretending to be asleep. He was fearful that midnight would come and the other boys would still be awake.

"We'd better go to sleep, too!" Harry said.

Bert yawned. "You're right! Night, Harry!"

"Night, Bert!"

Soon the two boys were sound asleep, and a few minutes later Freddie heard Nan and Dorothy go into their cabin. How slowly the hours seemed to pass as he kept checking the clock! Ten. Eleven. The little boy struggled to keep his eyelids from closing. He heard his parents and Dinah moving around, but finally it all was silent on the houseboat.

To Freddie's relief, Snap was shut out on deck. This had been done recently so the dog could watch for any intruders who might come aboard.

"Now he won't follow Flossie and me and bark," Freddie thought.

A few minutes before twelve, the little boy crept from his bunk and put on bathrobe and slippers. Tiptoeing across the cabin, he opened the door cautiously. He was happy to see Flossie leaving her room, too.

Without speaking, the small twins, their flash-lights beamed ahead of them, walked toward the storage locker. Reaching it, Freddie whispered:

"Floss, you sit on the right side here and I'll stand on the left. Maybe Bruce will come out."

"All right," Flossie whispered back. "But we'd better turn off our lights."

Five minutes . . . ten minutes . . . Flossie and Freddie were getting very sleepy sitting in the darkness of the deserted corridor.

Then suddenly they heard a little noise, no louder than the patter of a raindrop on a win-dowpane. Freddie leaned close to Flossie.

"Hear that, Flossie?"

"Yes!" she said, instantly alert.

At that moment the door of the storage locker squeaked ever so slightly. It was opening.

The twins felt chills go up and down their spines. But they bravely switched on their flash-lights. A boy's face was staring at them from the door opening!

"Bruce Watson!" Flossie cried hoarsely. Even though she had hoped to find him, Flossie was still surprised.

"Oh!" the startled runaway said, blinking in the light.

He started to duck back through the opening, but Freddie pulled him forward with all his strength.

"It's Flossie and me. We won't hurt you, Bruce!" he whispered.

Freddie finally persuaded the boy to stay with them, and led him down the corridor into the galley. Flossie shut the door quietly, so no one would hear them.

Turning on the ceiling light, she looked at Bruce closely. His shirt and pants were soiled and his face dirty. He looked uncomfortable and frightened.

"Don't be scared," Flossie said encouragingly.

"But I—I won't go back to my stepfather!" he declared, though he did not raise his voice.

"Maybe you won't have to," said Freddie. "Say, how long have you been on board?"

Bruce, convinced then that the twins meant to help him, told his story. He had stowed away the night Mr. Hardman had given him the whipping, unable to stand such treatment any longer. In the hold of the *Bluebird* he had removed a loose board, behind which was a hidden stairway. This led to the storage closet.

"Were you our ghost food taker?" Flossie asked suddenly.

"Yes," Bruce admitted, looking ashamed. "But I meant to get off in Brighthaven and from there try to find my uncle. My chance came when everyone left the houseboat at Brighthaven except Dinah. She went to clean the main cabin. But just as I started to sneak off, a boy climbed on board carrying a box of mice."

"Danny!" Flossie interrupted, looking at her twin.

Freddie nodded and Bruce continued with his story. It seemed that soon afterward everyone returned to the houseboat and he could not get off. He had not had another opportunity since then to leave unseen.

"You must be hungry, Bruce!" Flossie said kindly, looking at the thin boy.

"I sure am!" he replied. "I haven't eaten very much since I left home."

As Flossie and Freddie rummaged in the refrigerator, they smiled to think everyone had been blaming Captain McGinty all this time. They fixed Bruce a hearty plate of thick ham sandwiches, applesauce, some tomatoes, and a glass of milk.

Then the three children sat down and Bruce, munching on a sandwich, declared nothing had ever tasted so good! Resuming his story, the boy told how once he had almost been trapped in the locker, when Mr. Bobbsey tried to open it. In his hurry to get away, Bruce had caught his hand beneath a loose board. It hurt so much that he cried during part of the night.

"So you were the one I heard crying!" Flossie exclaimed. "We decided it was Snoop."

After Bruce had satisfied his hunger, he said

he would like to hide aboard the *Bluebird* until they stopped in Brighthaven. Then he would get off when no one was looking.

"But you don't have to hide any more," said Freddie.

"Oh yes, I do," Bruce insisted. "If I don't, the captain or your father or the police will send me back to Mr. Hardman. You mustn't tell! You must keep my secret!"

Flossie and Freddie did not know what to do. They knew their father wanted to protect Bruce, but they could not be sure of how Captain McGinty would feel about it.

Finally the small twins agreed not to say anything. "We'll sneak you food," Flossie promised. "Here's some to start." She loaded him down with provisions.

They watched Bruce climb back through the storage locker and down the secret stairway. Then the twins tiptoed quietly to their cabins.

Next morning, Dinah was the first to awaken and after dressing, she went to the galley to start breakfast. Intending to make a large ham omelet which Mrs. Bobbsey had ordered, Dinah was shocked to discover the platter on which she had placed the ham half empty.

"Mrs. Bobbsey!" she called, running up the corridor and knocking on Mrs. Bobbsey's cabin door. "Part of my ham disappeared last night!"

Hastily dressing, Mrs. Bobbsey rushed to the

galley, where the upset cook showed her the gouged-out meat and said a large quantity of other food was gone too.

"This is very strange," the twins' mother said.

"We took the food, Dinah!" called Freddie, appearing in the doorway with Flossie. The twins had heard Dinah's voice and decided to admit the theft to protect Bruce.

"We got up in the middle of the night," Flossie added.

Mrs. Bobbsey looked at her children unbelievingly. "You couldn't possibly have eaten all the food that's missing. 'Fess up now. What did you do with it?"

Freddie and Flossie looked at each other. What should they do—own up and maybe get Bruce into serious trouble?

Suddenly a voice behind them interrupted. "I took your food! Don't punish Flossie and Freddie!"

Scared, but determined to take the consequences, Bruce Watson stood in the doorway!

CHAPTER XXII

THE HAPPY STOWAWAY

"WHY, Bruce Watson!" Mrs. Bobbsey exclaimed, recognizing the boy instantly despite his dirty face and clothes. "Where did you come from?"

Dinah held up her hands in amazement. "Oh me, oh my, the ghost is a live one!" she cried.

The excitement brought everyone aboard the *Bluebird* on the run. What a surprise! As Bruce repeated his story, Bert told himself he had not been wrong in thinking the boy was aboard.

"We're sorry about your trouble and will help you all we can," said Mrs. Bobbsey. "Now, Bruce, we'll give you a chance to clean up and then have breakfast. After that, we'll talk."

Bert and Harry showed Bruce where he could take a quick bath. Then Bert gave him some slacks, and Harry gave him a gay sport shirt. Though their clothes were too big for Bruce, he grinned cheerfully.

"It sure is grand to feel clean again," he said as they went to the table.

Soon Dinah carried in platters filled with waffles and sausages, and Bruce's eyes widened. "Golly! That sure looks good!" he said.

After breakfast Mr. and Mrs. Bobbsey and the captain assured Bruce that they would not ask him to go back to his stepfather's farm, and the boy looked greatly relieved.

"Tell Bruce what you found out about him in Lemby," suggested Nan, and Mr. Bobbsey explained to the boy that his stepfather had no hold on him, because he had never legally adopted him.

"Thank goodness," said Bruce. "Now I *must* find my uncle."

"We'll look, too," said Flossie.

Freddie begged to try out the secret stairway, so Bruce showed the others where it was.

"How ever did you discover this hiding place?" Nan asked curiously.

Bruce stared at her in a puzzled manner. "I knew it must be here. A boat I used to play on when I was little had a place like it."

"A houseboat?" Nan asked.

"I guess so. I don't remember."

"Do you think it had anything to do with your uncle?" Bert questioned. "If it did, maybe it'll help us find him."

Bruce thought hard but could recall nothing further. "But maybe I will," he said hopefully.

Mrs. Bobbsey suggested that during the trip

to Brighthaven the children forget the subject
and just have fun. First they showed Bruce the
Indian treasures they had found, saying they
were hoping that the curator at the museum
would tell them the things had once belonged
to Ko-sa-mia and White Fawn.

Then Freddie suggested some games. "We'll
play, 'Let's Pretend!'" he announced.

"I'll be a butterfly!" Flossie said, and danced
around the deck, moving her arms like wings.

"I'm a bee and I'm going to sting you!"
laughed Dorothy. "Bzzzzzzzzz!"

"What are you, Bruce?" asked Nan kindly,
sensing that he did not understand the game. "An
animal or an insect?"

Bruce thought a minute. "I'd like to be a sea
gull," he said finally. "I used to watch them on
the beach when I was little."

Suddenly his face lighted up and he cried,
"That's it! I remember now! My uncle John
did have a boat and he named it the *Sea Gull*
because I liked them so much."

The children stared in amazement, and Bert
urged, "Keep thinking, Bruce! What town did
you live in?"

"I can't seem to remember any more."

"Back in Lemby you told us something about
palm trees and a beach," said Nan. "And that
your uncle did live down South. Could it have
been Florida, Bruce?"

The boy shook his head unhappily. "I don't know. Maybe it was."

"I have an idea," said Bert. "The man we bought this boat from just came up from Florida. He might know about the *Sea Gull.*"

"Let's ask Dad what he thinks!" cried Nan, seeing her father walking down the steps from the wheelhouse.

Mr. Bobbsey listened thoughtfully to their story. "I think you have a good idea," he said. "Mr. Enslow is staying at a hotel in Lakeport. I'll call him from Brighthaven."

Bruce and his new friends could hardly wait to dock there. But when they arrived, it seemed best for the stowaway to remain aboard until Mr. Bobbsey had made his calls. The boy willingly remained with Mrs. Bobbsey and Dinah.

The others hurried uptown, carrying the golden arrow and the other Indian treasures. Their first stop was the museum where the curator carefully examined the articles. Bert told where they had been found.

"Could they have been Ko-sa-mia's?" he asked eagerly.

"Yes, I'm sure they were," the man said. "This is the missing link in the story about them. Children, you're to be congratulated. I hope," he added, "that you will give these to this museum. They are rare and valuable."

The children glanced at one another, then

suddenly Flossie said, "It was really our dog that found the cave and I know he'll be glad to give them to you."

Everyone laughed and Mr. Bobbsey said, "I guess that settles it. We'll leave the treasures here."

"And now let's call Mr. Enslow," Freddie urged, pointing to a telephone booth in the lobby of the museum.

As Mr. Bobbsey put in a call to Mr. Enslow, the *Bluebird*'s former owner, the children crowded around the booth. They heard Mr. Bobbsey gasp.

"What's that you say, Mr. Enslow?" he asked. Then he listened some more and wrote something on a piece of paper.

Finishing the conversation, he left the booth and told the excited children an interesting story. Mr. Enslow had purchased the houseboat from a man named John Borden, who lived in a coastal town in Florida. Mr. Borden had called the boat the *Sea Gull*. Mr. Enslow had changed its name to the *Bluebird*.

"It may be a coincidence," said Mr. Bobbsey, "but it's just possible that John Borden is Bruce's uncle. I have Mr. Borden's phone number and will call his home right away."

The Bobbsey twins and their cousins waited breathlessly. Minutes passed before the long-distance call was put through. Finally a man's voice answered on the Florida end of the wire. Mr. Bobbsey identified himself and asked:

"Have you a nephew by the name of Bruce Watson?"

"Have I!" Mr. Borden exclaimed, loudly enough for the children to hear. "I've been trying to get in touch with him for the past three years! Do you know where he is?"

"Indeed I do." The rest the young listeners could not hear.

As Mr. Bobbsey came out of the booth a few minutes later, the children clamored to learn the result of the conversation.

"I think Bruce should be the first to hear," Mr. Bobbsey declared, and though the others were bursting with curiosity, they agreed.

Bruce, seeing them coming, ran down the gangplank. Captain McGinty and Dinah followed. "Tell me, please!" he begged.

"You're going to be happy at this news, Bruce!" the twins' father smiled. "I spoke to your uncle, John Borden. You also have an Aunt Ruth and a little cousin Charlie, who is five years old."

"Oh, Mr. Bobbsey!" said Bruce in a joyful voice. "Tell me more about them!"

The twins' father explained that when Mr. Borden heard of the death of Bruce's mother, he had written Mr. Hardman, offering to take care of Bruce. Mr. Hardman had written back that he loved the little boy and would give him a good home.

"But he didn't!" Bruce burst out.

Continuing, Mr. Bobbsey said that Mr. Borden and his family had moved to Cuba after that and lived there for several years. During this time he frequently wrote Mr. Hardman concerning Bruce. The letters had come back marked, "Address Unknown."

"I'll bet your stepfather sent back Mr. Borden's letters!" Bert said angrily. "What do you think, Bruce?"

The bewildered boy nodded his head thoughtfully. "I guess so! And all that time I thought my uncle had forgotten about me."

"And now for the best news of all," Mr. Bobbsey said. "Mr. and Mrs. Borden and your cousin Charlie are flying up and will meet you in Lakeport when we get there. They will take you back to Florida to live with them!"

"Hurray!" shouted Freddie, and Bert added, "Now Mr. Hardman can't blame Dad any longer for Bruce's leaving the farm."

Bruce's face glowed like a Christmas tree light. "You mean I'll really have a nice family of my own—just like you Bobbseys?" he asked. "Oh, thank you, thank you!"

"But I was hoping Bruce would stay with us for a while!" Flossie pouted.

"Me, too!" added Dinah. "It sure don't leave

me much time to fatten him up. But I'm glad he's going to have a good home now!"

"We all are!" the others shouted.

At this point, Captain McGinty stepped forward. "Bruce," he said, "I hereby promote you from the rank of stowaway to deck officer of the

Bluebird." And, with a smile, he pulled a yachting cap from under his coat and placed it on the boy's head.

Cheers of delight went up from everyone, and as the group returned to the houseboat, the happy stowaway walked as though his feet were light as feathers.